James Hadley Chase and The Murder Room

>>> This title is part of The Murder Room, our series dedicated to making available out-of-print or hard-to-find titles by classic crime writers.

Crime fiction has always held up a mirror to society. The Victorians were fascinated by sensational murder and the emerging science of detection; now we are obsessed with the forensic detail of violent death. And no other genre has so captivated and enthralled readers.

Vast troves of classic crime writing have for a long time been unavailable to all but the most dedicated frequenters of second-hand bookshops. The advent of digital publishing means that we are now able to bring you the backlists of a huge range of titles by classic and contemporary crime writers, some of which have been out of print for decades.

From the genteel amateur private eyes of the Golden Age and the femmes fatales of pulp fiction, to the morally ambiguous hard-boiled detectives of mid twentieth-century America and their descendants who walk our twenty-first century streets, The Murder Room has it all. **>>>**

The Murder Room
Where Criminal Minds Meet

themurderroom.com

James Hadley Chase (1906–1985)

Born René Brabazon Raymond in London, the son of a British colonel in the Indian Army, James Hadley Chase was educated at King's School in Rochester, Kent, and left home at the age of 18. He initially worked in book sales until, inspired by the rise of gangster culture during the Depression and by reading James M. Cain's *The Postman Always Rings Twice*, he wrote his first novel, *No Orchids for Miss Blandish*. Despite the American setting of many of his novels, Chase (like Peter Cheyney, another hugely successful British noir writer) never lived there, writing with the aid of maps and a slang dictionary. He had phenomenal success with the novel, which continued unabated throughout his entire career, spanning 45 years and nearly 90 novels. His work was published in dozens of languages and more than thirty titles were adapted for film. He served in the RAF during World War II, where he also edited the RAF Journal. In 1956 he moved to France with his wife and son; they later moved to Switzerland, where Chase lived until his death in 1985.

No Orchids for Miss Blandish
Eve
More Deadly Than the Male
Mission to Venice
Mission to Siena
Not Safe to Be Free
Shock Treatment
Come Easy – Go Easy

You Must Be Kidding
A Can of Worms
Try This One for Size
You Can Say That Again
Hand Me a Fig Leaf
Have a Nice Night
We'll Share a Double Funeral
Not My Thing
Hit Them Where It Hurts

Shock Treatment

James Hadley Chase

An Orion book

Copyright © Hervey Raymond 1959

The right of James Hadley Chase to be identified as the author of this
work has been asserted in accordance with the Copyright, Designs and
Patents Act 1988.

This edition published by
The Orion Publishing Group Ltd
Orion House
5 Upper St Martin's Lane
London WC2H 9EA

An Hachette UK company
A CIP catalogue record for this book is available from the British Library

ISBN 978 1 4719 0338 0

www.orionbooks.co.uk

Chapter I

ALL this I am to tell you about could probably never have happened in any other town except Glyn Camp.

Situated in the Californian hill district, Glyn Camp is one of those tiny Rip van Winkle summer resorts where writers, artists and those on pension make their homes in the peace and beauty of a district not all that far from the fun and games of the Pacific Coast.

I rented a reasonably comfortable cabin up in this district, and from the cabin, I ran a radio and television sales and service organization.

By road, my cabin was four miles from Glyn Camp, and once a week I drove into town to get my groceries, and then I would go along to Sheriff Jefferson's office for a talk and a shot of his apple-jack which he manufactured himself.

Sheriff Jefferson has an important part in this story so I'd better say something about him now. He had been sheriff of Glyn Camp for the best part of fifty years. No one knew exactly how old he was, but it was agreed by those who had lived longest in the town that he was over eighty. He knew, and the town knew, that he was beyond his job, but that didn't prevent the town electing him sheriff again when election time came around nor did it prevent him from taking on the new term. Glyn Camp without Sheriff Jefferson was as unthinkable as New York without the Statue of Liberty.

The other character in Glyn Camp I must mention before I go any further is Doc Mallard.

Doc Mallard had been practising medicine for as long as Sheriff Jefferson had been administering the law. He was the only doctor in Glyn Camp, which was a notoriously healthy spot, and he seldom had anything to do. Anyone who happened to be seriously ill or who was about to produce a baby went wisely to Los Angeles State Hospital, some eighty miles down the mountain road.

1

Doc Mallard still had a handful of faithful patients; but they were dying off fast, and he now spent most of his time playing checkers with Sheriff Jefferson or sitting on the verandah of his shabby little cabin, staring emptily at the view.

On this hot summer morning I was down in town to pick up a TV set. After I had loaded the set onto my truck I went over to Jefferson's office for the routine gossip.

We had a drink together and discussed this and that. After a while I said I had to get up to Blue Jay lake and I'd look in again next time I was in town.

'If you're going up to Blue Jay lake, son,' Jefferson said, leaning back in his rocking chair, 'there's a chance for some new business for you. I hear there's new people in Mr Williams's cabin: a married couple. The man's a cripple. He goes around in a wheel chair. I should imagine he'd be interested to have a TV up there.'

'I'll call on him,' I said, taking out my reminder book. 'Do you know his name?'

'Jack Delaney.'

'I'll look him up on my way home.'

A cripple who lived in a wheel chair seemed to me to be a natural for a TV set. As soon as I had installed the radio I had just sold to one of my customers, I drove over to Blue Jay cabin.

I had been up there a couple of years back and remembered the place as a small but luxurious dwelling, with a magnificent view of the mountains, the valley below and the sea in the far distance.

At the top of the narrow lane was a gate. I had to get off the truck to open the gate, and then drive up the smooth tarmac road that led to the cabin that seemed to be clinging to the mountain side the way a fly clings to a wall.

There was a big glittering Buick estate wagon standing before the steps leading up to the verandah and I pulled up behind it.

A man sat in a wheel chair on the verandah. He was smoking a cigar, an open magazine on his knees.

He was around forty-five to fifty, a little overweight. There was that pinched, bitter look about his fleshy face of a cripple

2

who has suffered, and his grey eyes were hard and cold.

I got off the truck and walked up the steps onto the verandah.

'Mr Delaney?'

He stared suspiciously at me.

'That's my name. What do you want?'

'I heard you had just moved in, and as I was passing, I thought I'd see if I could fix you up with a radio or a TV set,' I said.

'Television? You can't get any worth-while reception up amongst these mountains,' he said, staring at me.

'With the right aerial, you'd get first-rate reception up here, Mr Delaney,' I said.

'Don't tell me,' he said. 'Not with these mountains screening the beam.'

'Give me five minutes, Mr Delaney,' I said, 'and I'll prove to you I'm not wasting your time nor mine either.'

I went down to the truck and hauled off a small TV set, carried it up onto the verandah and set it on a table near him.

He put down his magazine and watched me as I got the special aerial I carried around with me from the truck.

Within seven minutes I had a picture on the screen that was as sharp and as clear and as free from interference as any picture you could wish to see.

It was my good luck they were showing a fight film. I learned later that Delaney was a fanatical fight fan. I saw at once the picture had caught his interest. He leaned forward, his face losing some of its bitterness as he stared at the lighted screen.

He watched the fight to the end. It lasted twenty minutes. It was a good meaty scrap with a couple of heavyweights pounding the daylights out of each other. One of them finally hung a bone crusher on the other's jaw and, by the way he went down, I knew he wouldn't get up inside the count, and he didn't.

'How's that for reception?' I asked, moving around so I could face him.

3

'I wouldn't have believed it,' Delaney said. 'It's damned good. What's the price of this thing?'

I told him.

'Isn't there anything better?'

'Well, yes: there are plenty better. Would you be interested in a set that has a TV, radio receiver and VHF?'

He leaned back in his chair and stared at me. There was an arrogant expression in his eyes that irritated me.

'Who did you say you were?' he asked.

'Terry Regan,' I said. 'I look after the district for TV and radio.'

'Maybe I should go to one of the big dealers in LA,' he said musingly. 'I don't care to deal with a one-man outfit. When I buy something, I buy the best.'

'That's up to you, Mr Delaney,' I said, 'but if you want the best, then it has to be hand-made. That's something I specialize in. I could build you a set that would give you quality plus. It would include a twenty-five-inch screen TV set, an FM and radio tuner, a recorder player and a tape recorder. I'd also give you an electrostatic speaker as a separate unit.'

'Could you make a set like that?' His unbelieving, contemptuous tone riled me. 'How do I know it would be any good?'

'I'm not asking you to take my word for it. I made a set along those lines for Mr Hamish, the writer, who lives a couple of miles from here. You have only to call him and he'll tell you how satisfied he is with it.'

Delaney shrugged his shoulders.

'Oh, I'll take your word for it,' he said. 'What would a set like that cost?'

'Depending on the kind of cabinet you want,' I said, 'I could do you something first class for fifteen hundred dollars.' I heard a slight sound behind me, and for no reason at all, I had a queer, creepy sensation that crawled up my spine and into the roots of my hair.

I turned.

A woman stood in the doorway, and she was looking directly at me.

4

II

My first sight of Gilda Delaney is something I'm never likely to forget.

She was a little above medium height with a golden tan complexion that comes from hours out in the sun. Her hair was the colour of polished bronze and reached to her shoulders. Her eyes were big and as blue as forget-me-nots, and there was that look in them that a man, who is anything of a man, must react to, the way a fighting bull reacts when the matador flicks his cape in the moment of incitement.

She was wearing a red cowboy shirt and a pair of blue jeans, and what that combination did to show off her shape was something to see.

Delaney glanced around and stared at her, then he said in a flat, indifferent tone, 'This is my wife.' He made it sound as if she was of no consequence. Looking at her, he went on, 'This is Mr Regan. He's the TV and radio man around here. He's trying to sell me a TV set.'

'Isn't that just what you want?' she said. She had one of those low, husky voices that went with her shape and the look in her eyes.

'It could be.' He stubbed out his cigar, then looked over at me. 'Suppose I don't care for this set you propose to build? What happens then?'

'If you don't care for it, Mr Delaney,' I said, having to make an effort to keep my mind on business, aware of this woman as I had never been aware of any other woman before, 'then I guess I'll find someone else who'll buy it, but I think you will care for it.'

The woman said, 'You could get a lot of fun out of a TV set. You should have it.'

She nodded to me, her forget-me-not blue eyes moving over me inquisitively, then with a faint smile that meant nothing, she passed me and went down the steps, along the path and out of sight as she rounded the corner of the cabin.

I watched her until I lost sight of her. If you had been able to see the way she walked, the smooth roll of her hips, the power that was in her body, her upright carriage, you would

5

have felt the same way as I felt, and I mean just exactly that. Right at that moment, watching her as she moved down the steps, and along the concrete path, I wanted her more than I had ever wanted any other woman before.

Delaney said, 'Well, okay, Regan, make the set. If I like it, I'll buy it.'

I dragged my attention back to business.

Not a very satisfactory way of doing business, I thought; this guy sitting in his wheel chair could be a bluffer and a phoney. I could use up quite a bit of my savings building him a super set and he could slide out of buying it by saying he didn't like it. But I wasn't going to argue with him. I wanted to see her again, and this was the way I could see her again.

'Well, okay,' I said, 'I'll build it. It'll take a couple of weeks. In the meantime you would probably like to have this set to carry on with.'

'Yes, leave it here,' he said. 'I'll pay you rent for it.'

'You don't have to do that. I'll be happy to leave it on loan. You'll need a permanent aerial. I'll be out tomorrow to fix it for you. Will that be all right?'

'Sure,' he said. 'Come out tomorrow. I'm always around.'

I left him sitting on the verandah, staring at the lighted screen of the TV set. As I drove down the tarmac I kept my eyes open for her, but she didn't show.

I had her on my mind all the way back to the cabin. She was still in my mind when I went to bed that night, and she was with me when I got up and began to put my breakfast together.

I went out to Blue Jay cabin the following afternoon. I made it the afternoon because I thought there might be a chance she would be out shopping in the morning and I didn't intend to miss seeing her.

Delaney was sitting on the verandah with the TV set on. He was watching a gangster film and he scarcely bothered to look up as I got off the truck.

I collected the aerial I had brought with me, a roll of flex and my tool kit, and I walked up the steps.

'Go on in,' he said, waving to the lounge. 'You'll find the

servant or my wife somewhere.'

The way he said it the servant and his wife were of a kind, and that riled me.

I went into the big living-room that was as luxurious and as expensive as only a millionaire could make it.

I set down the stuff I had brought with me and, seeing no one, I crossed to the double doors, opened them and looked out onto a patio with a miniature fountain in the centre full of gold fish exercising themselves in the sun.

I walked through a doorway on the far side of the patio and into a big hall from which several doors led.

One of the doors stood open and I heard Gilda Delaney humming softly to herself.

'Mrs Delaney,' I said, slightly raising my voice.

She came to the door. She was even better than the image I had been keeping of her in my mind during the past thirty-six hours. No memory could recapture the look she had, nor the sensual quality of her body, nor the way her bronze hair glinted in the sunlight coming through the big open window.

She had on a cream silk shirt and a pleated sky-blue skirt. The sight of her set my heart thumping.

'Hello, Mr Regan,' she said, and she smiled.

'Your husband told me to come on in,' I said, and my voice sounded husky. 'I want to fix the aerial. Is there a way up to the roof?'

'There's an attic and a skylight. You will want the steps. They are in the storeroom: that door there'; and she pointed.

'Thanks,' I said and paused, then went on, 'Looks like the set is a success.'

She nodded, and I was aware her eyes were going over me, thoughtfully, probingly, as if she were asking herself what kind of man I was.

'It is, He put it on at nine this morning, and it has been on ever since.'

'For someone tied to a chair the way he is,' I said, 'there's nothing like a TV set.'

'Of course.' A faintly bored expression appeared in her forget-me-not blue eyes. 'Well, I mustn't hold you up.'

7

It was a little nudging hint that I had work to do and she didn't want to stand gossiping all the afternoon.

'I'll get on. That door there?'

'Yes.'

'And the attic?'

'Over there. There's a trap up to it'.

'Well, thanks, Mrs Delaney.'

I got the steps from the storeroom, stood them under the trap, climbed the steps and pushed the trap open.

The attic roof was just high enough for me to stand up in, and the skylight gave me easy access to the roof. I opened the skylight and then descended to the ground floor.

I went back into the lounge, collected my kit and the aerial and started back along the passage. As I passed her door, she appeared in the doorway.

There was an expression in her eyes that stopped me as if I had walked into a brick wall.

'Do you want any help?' she asked.

'Thanks, but I don't want to bother you.'

'I have nothing to do if I can be of help.'

We looked at each other.

'Well, I'd be glad then. I don't like taking my tool kit out on a roof. If you could hand me up what I want, it would be a real help.'

'That sounds easy enough.'

She moved with that liquid grace that had held my attention before. She paused by the steps.

'Do you think you can get up there?' I said, nodding to the open trap.

'I think so if you will hold the steps steady.'

I set down the aerial and joined her. She was wearing a perfume that I didn't know: heady stuff that went with her character and personality. Standing this close to her really got me going.

I put my hand on the steps.

'They're safe enough,' I said.

She started up them. Half way up, she paused and looked

8

down at me. Her long, slim legs were on the level with my eyes.

'I should be wearing jeans for this kind of work,' she said, and smiled.

'That's okay,' I said, and it sounded as if I had a plum in my mouth. 'I won't look.'

She laughed.

'I hope you won't.'

She put her hands on each side of the trap, then swung herself nimbly up into the attic.

Her pleated skirt billowed out, and the brief glimpse I got of her as I looked up set my blood racing.

She looked down at me through the trap opening. From that angle she really looked more than something with her bronze-coloured hair hanging forward, framing her face.

Her eyes searched my face with that knowledgeable, cool appraisal of a woman who knows all about men and how men will react to what she knew I had just seen.

'If you'll give me the aerial . . .' she said.

I was glad of the excuse to turn away and pick up the aerial. I handed it up to her, then the tool kit and then the coil of flex.

I climbed up beside her.

In that hot, stuffy little attic we suddenly seemed to be the only two people left in the world. Up there I couldn't hear the TV. I couldn't hear anything except the thump-thump-thump of my heart-beats.

'I'm glad I don't have to go out there,' she said, moving away from me to stare through the skylight at the patch of blue sky. 'I haven't any head for heights.'

'I used to feel that way, but it doesn't bother me now. I guess one gets used to anything if you try hard enough.'

'I used to think that too, but not now. I know my husband will never get used to sitting in his chair for the rest of his days.'

I began to uncoil the flex.

'That's different. Did he have an accident?'

'Yes.' She lifted her hair off her shoulders, letting it run

9

through her slim-waisted fingers. 'He feels it terribly. I think it's worse for him than most men. He was the tennis coach for the Pacific Film Studios. He coached all the famous stars. It was a glamorous and very paying job. He is close on fifty. You wouldn't think he could be a great tennis player, not at that age, but he was. He had so much fun and he loved teaching. That was really all he was ever good at. He had no other interests. Then this accident happened. He'll never be able to walk again.'

And he'll never be able to make love to you again either, I thought. If there was any pity in my thoughts, it was for her.

'That's tough,' I said. 'Isn't there something he could interest himself in? He's not planning to sit in that chair and do nothing for the rest of his days, is he?'

'Yes. He made an awful lot of money. That's something we're not short of.' Her red, full lips twisted into a bitter smile. 'He has come out here to get away from his friends. The one thing he hates more than anything is to be pitied.'

I fixed the stripped ends of the flex to the aerial leads.

'How about you? It can't be much fun being buried out here, can it?'

She lifted her shoulders.

'He is my husband.' She studied me for a long moment, then said, 'Shall I hold it now?'

That broke up the conversation. I got out onto the roof and she passed the aerial up to me.

With her helping me, it didn't take long to fix the aerial in place. She handed up the tools I wanted, and every time I came to the skylight and looked down at her, I became more aware of her.

'That's it,' I said, and swung myself down through the skylight into the attic.

'It didn't take long,' she said.

She was standing close to me.

'I've put up so many aerials I could put one up in my sleep.' I was beginning to breathe fast again.

I knew she wasn't listening, She was looking intently at me, her chin up, and there was that thing lighting up her eyes.

10

Suddenly she swayed towards me.

I grabbed her.

In the past I have kissed quite a few women, but this was different. This was the kind of kiss you dream about. She melted into me: it was the moment of truth - there is no other way of describing it.

We clung to each other for maybe twenty or thirty seconds, then she broke free and stepped back and put her finger on her lips, pressing them while she stared at me. Her forget-me-not blue eyes had turned cloudy and were half closed, and she was breathing as fast as I was.

'There's lipstick on your mouth,' she said in that husky, spooky voice of hers; then, turning, she reached the trap opening, and swung herself out of my sight.

I stood there trembling, aware of the thudding of my heart while I listened to her quick-light footfalls as she went away from me.

III

I got back to my cabin around eight o'clock in the evening; my mind still full of Gilda. I sat on the verandah, lit a cigarette and did some thinking.

I kept asking myself why she had kissed me.

I said to myself: a woman as lovely as she is with her background of luxury is not going to take you seriously. That was an off-beat moment. You've got to get it out of your mind. It's something that won't happen again. Don't try to kid yourself into believing she would leave her husband for you. What have you to offer her anyway? This lousy little cabin? You couldn't keep her in stockings. It was an off-beat moment, and she meant nothing by it.

Then suddenly, breaking into my thoughts, the telephone bell began to ring.

I got up and went into the lounge and took up the receiver.

'I hope I'm not disturbing you, Mr Regan.'

There was only one soft, husky voice like that in the world. At the sound of it I had a rush of blood to my head.

'Why, no. . . .'

'I wanted to see you. I suppose I couldn't come over to, your place about eleven?'

'Why ... yes....'

'Then at eleven,' and she hung up.

A minute or so after eleven, I saw the headlights of her car coming up the dirt track and I got to my feet.

My heart was thumping as I walked down the steps and watched the estate wagon drive up the rough drive-in.

She pulled up outside the cabin and came towards me.

'I'm sorry to be so late, Mr Regan,' she said, 'but I had to wait until my husband was in bed.'

That made it a conspiracy. I was breathing fast and I was pretty worked up.

'Won't you come up onto the *verandah, Mrs Delaney?*'

She moved past me and up onto the verandah.

I had turned the lights off, and the only light came from the lounge, making a rectangle of light on the floor of the verandah.

She moved across this patch of light. She had changed into her slacks and the cowboy shirt. She walked to one of the old basket chairs and sat down.

'I want to apologize for what happened this afternoon.' She seemed very calm and matter-of-fact. 'You must be thinking I am one of those uncontrolled women who throw themselves at any man.'

'Of course I don't,' I said, sitting down near her. 'It was my fault. I shouldn't have...'

'Please don't be insincere. It's always the woman's fault when a thing like that happens. I just happened to lose my head for the moment.' She shifted lower in the chair. 'Could I have a cigarette?'

I took out my case and offered it.

She took a cigarette. I struck a match. My hand was so unsteady, she put her fingers on my wrist so she could light the cigarette. The touch of her cool flesh on mine increased the thud of my heart-beats.

'I'm ashamed of myself,' she went on, leaning back in the chair. 'It is hard sometimes for a woman in my position. After

12

all, why make a mystery of it? But I should have controlled myself. I thought it was only fair to you to come here and explain.'

'You needn't have ... I wasn't imagining...'

'Of course you were. I know I am attractive to men. It's something I can't do anything about, and when certain men find out about my husband being a cripple, they begin to pester me. Up to now I haven't met a man attractive enough to bother me, and it has been easy to hold them off.' She paused, drawing on her cigarette. 'But there's something about you. . . .' She broke off and lifted her hands, letting them fall back onto the arms of the chair. 'Anyway, I had to come here and tell you it isn't going to happen again. You see, Mr Regan, if I were unlucky enough to fall in love with another man, I could never leave my husband. He is a cripple. He relies on me. I have a conscience about him.'

'If you did happen to fall in love with another man,' I said, 'no one could blame you for leaving your husband. You're young. He can't expect you to remain tied to him for the rest of his days. It would be throwing your life away.'

'Do you think so? When I married him I promised to take him for better or for worse. Sliding out through a back door would be impossible to me. Besides, I was responsible for the accident that crippled him. That's why, apart from the ethics of my marriage vows, I have a conscience about him.'

'You were responsible?'

'Yes.' She crossed her long, slim legs. 'You are the first person I have met since the accident I feel I can talk to. Would it bore you if I told you about the accident?'

'Nothing you say to me would ever bore me.'

'Thank you.' She paused, then went on, 'Jack and I have been married for four years. Three months after we were married the accident happened.' Her voice now sounded impersonal and wooden. 'We had been to a party. Jack had been drinking. I hated him to drive when he was lit up, and he was often lit up. When we got into the car, I insisted on driving. We quarrelled about it, but finally I got my way. We were on a mountain road. The movement of the car lulled Jack to sleep. Half-way up the road I came to a stationary car that blocked the road. It belonged to a friend of ours. He had also been to the party. He had run out of gas. I pulled up and got out of the car and started to walk over to him. I had stopped on a very steep part of the road. As soon as I got out of the car, it began to move backwards. I couldn't have set the parking brake properly.' She flicked her half-finished cigarette into the garden. 'Jack was still asleep. I rushed back, but it was too late. The car went off the road. I shall never forget that moment, listening to the terrible noise as the car crashed down the mountain side. If I had put the parking brake on properly, it would never have happened.'

'It was an accident,' I said. 'It could have happened to anyone.'

'Jack doesn't think so. He thinks it was entirely my fault.

I have the most horrible guilt complex about it, and that is why I can never leave him.'

I asked her the question I had to know.

'Do you still love him?'

I saw her stiffen.

'Love him? That doesn't come into it. I've lived with him now for four years. He has suffered a lot, and he isn't very pleasant to live with. He drinks, and his temper can be hateful. He is twenty-three years older than I am. His ideas are not my ideas, but I married him and I have to accept him. It was through me that he is a cripple and his life has been spoilt.'

'It was an accident,' I said, gripping my clenched fists between my knees. 'You can't blame yourself for what happened.'

'So what do you think I should do?'

'You are free to leave him if you want to. That's the way I see it.'

'But then you haven't got my conscience.' She held out her hand and I gave her a cigarette. I left my chair to light the cigarette. In the light of the match flame we stared at each other. 'You are a disturbing person.' Her voice was very low.

'You're disturbing, too.'

'Yes, I know. I'm not only disturbing to most men, I'm

14

disturbing to myself. My life is difficult, Mr Regan. I think
perhaps you have already realized that. What we did this
afternoon has been worrying me a lot. Will you accept my
apologies?'

'You don't have to apologize. I understand.'

'I believe you do. I wouldn't have come out at this time of
night, alone, if I wasn't sure you would understand. I must get
back.'

She got up.

'It's nice out here and so quiet. I asked Maria, my maid
about you. She tells me you aren't married and you live alone.

'I've lived on my own out here for a long time.' I was
standing by her side now and we were both looking across the
heads of the trees, outlined in the moonlight.

'Do you mind living on your own? I should have thought
you would have married.'

'I haven't yet found the right woman.' She glanced at me.

The hard light of the moon fell directly on her face and I
could see a small, bitter smile on her mouth.

'Are you difficult to please?'

'I suppose so. Marriage is very permanent – at least it is to
me. I feel the way you do about it.'

'One must have love. I never really loved my husband. I
married him for security. Before I met him I had nothing. I
would be a lot happier now if I still had nothing except my
freedom.'

'You can still have your freedom.'

'Not now. If I left him, I'd have my conscience to torment
me. A conscience is a torment prison than anything else in the
world.'

'My conscience never bothers me, but I guess I can
understand about yours.'

'I don't know what I am going to think of myself tomorrow,'
she said, tracing her forefinger idly along the verandah rail. I
came out here on the spur of the moment. I wanted you to
understand....'

I put my hand over hers.

'Gilda . . .'

She turned and looked at me.... She was trembling.

'Gilda I'm crazy about you....'

'Oh, darling, I'm such a hypocrite,' she said breathlessly. 'I'm so ashamed, but the moment I saw you . . .'

I had her in my arms and her mouth was against mine. We clung to each other and I could feel the yearning, the crying out of her body as she pressed against me.

I picked her up in my arms and carried her into the cabin. The brown owl that always sits on the roof of the garage flew suddenly across the face of the moon.

It made a small, insignificant shadow.

Chapter II

I

SHE came to my cabin for three successive nights, and we made love.

It was hurried, furtive love, and after the first shock of excitement had passed, it was unsatisfactory love - anyway, for me.

She was frightened someone would see her coming or leaving my cabin. She was terrified her husband would find out she was being unfaithful to him.

So our love-making was furtive, and it worried me to find how jumpy she was, and how she would sit up abruptly on the bed, her fingers gripping my arm, when there was any unusual sound such as the occasional passing car, the hoot of the owl or the tapping on the roof from a branch of a tree.

Each of these three nights, she stayed with me for less than an hour. Our moments together consisted only of this desperate, violent love-making. We scarcely had time to talk before she wanted to get back to her home, and I knew as little about her now as I had done when I first met her.

16

But in spite of that, I was in love with her. For me, this union meant much more than the physical act of love. It bothered me to know that her husband had such a powerful influence over her.

If she talked about anything, it was about him. I didn't want to listen to what she had to say about him. I wanted her to talk about herself, and I longed for her to talk about me, but she didn't.

'I would never forgive myself if he found out,' she said as she dressed on the third night of our love-making. 'I keep thinking he might be wanting me. In the past, he has had nights of pain, and he has woken me to give him something to make him sleep. He could be calling for me now.'

'For God's sake, Gilda, get him out of your mind!' I was fast losing patience with her. 'Why don't you tell him the truth? Why don't you tell him you're in love with me and you must have your freedom?'

'But, Terry, I can never leave him. I'm responsible for the accident that spoilt his life. I could never, never leave him!' I pulled her to me.

'Do you love me, Gilda?'

She looked up at me, and there was that thing again in her eyes.

'Can you doubt it, Terry? Yes, I love you. I think of you every minute of the day. I long to be with you. It's a dreadful thing to say, but if only he were dead . . . then I could be with you as I want to be with you for always. I'll never be free until he is dead.'

'But he isn't likely to die, is he?' I said impatiently.

She pulled away from me and, moving to the window, she looked out onto the moonlit trees.

'No. When the doctor examined him before he came here, he said he was in splendid shape. He could easily last for another thirty years or more.'

'Well, then, why waste time wishing he were dead? We're not going to wait for thirty years, are we? You've got to ask him for a divorce!'

'I can't do it, Terry!' She looked up at me. 'How many more

17

times do I have to tell you I can't possibly leave him.'

'Of course you can! He has money. He could get a nurse to look after him. How much money do you think he has got?'

She lifted her shoulders.

'I don't know - a lot. A hundred and fifty thousand: perhaps more.'

'Well, then, he can afford to have someone to look after him, and you can have your freedom.'

She turned away from me.

'If he died, Terry,' she said in a low, distinct voice, 'that money would come to me. You and I would share it. What would you do with a hundred and fifty thousand dollars?'

'Why talk about it?'

'Terry, please! I'm asking you! What would you do with all that money?'

I suddenly began to think what I would do with such a sum if it were mine. The thought sent a creepy sensation up my spine.

'If I had that amount of capital,' I said, 'I could double it in a year. I would open a shop in Los Angeles. I would have three or maybe four service vans covering the whole district. I would specialize in hand-made Hi-Fi sets. I could make a whale of a lot of money.'

'You would love to do that, wouldn't you? And I would love to be at your side and see you do it.'

I stared at her.

'What's the sense of talking like this, Gilda? He's not going to die. You won't get the money until you are too old to get any fun out of it! So what? Get a divorce! Never mind about the money! Get your freedom!'

She shook her head.

'I can't get a divorce. I can't help this guilt complex of mine. It was my fault he became a cripple. I can't leave him now.'

I drew in a long breath of exasperation.

'So what do we do?'

She moved slowly out of the bedroom and into the lounge and I followed her. She paused on the verandah.

'What do we do, Terry?' she said, not looking at me. 'We

mustn't see each other again, that's what we do. It's as simple as that. The woman I despise most is the cheat. I have been despising myself ever since we began to make love. We must stop it. It's the only way. There is no other way. We must stop seeing each other.'

That gave me a hell of a jolt.

'Now, look...'

'I mean it, Terry.'

'Don't let's make hasty decisions. We'll talk about it tomorrow night. This is something . . .'

'There won't be a tomorrow night,' she said. 'I won't be coming tomorrow night. This has got to be stopped now.' I caught hold of her, but she broke free.

'No, please, don't make it harder for me, Terry. You don't imagine I like this any better than you do, but I know now how wicked I have been and I must stop it. I must go. We mustn't ever see each other again.'

There was such despair and truth in her voice that I stepped away from her, a sharp pain at my heart.

She ran down the verandah steps and across to the garage.

I remained there, watching her drive away, trying to tell myself that she couldn't mean what she said, that it was only her conscience bothering her, and that tomorrow night I would see her again.

But she didn't come.

The following night I sat on the verandah waiting for her, and as the hands of my watch moved around to half past twelve, I knew she wouldn't be coming.

That made me feel pretty bad.

The following day was Friday: the day she always went into Glyn Camp to do the week's shopping.

I was down there, waiting for her.

But she didn't come.

After a while I began to prowl up and down the main street looking for her, but I didn't see her.

Finally, at twelve o'clock, I had to accept the bitter fact that she wasn't coming, and I headed back to the parking lot feeling depressed enough to cut my throat.

19

As I reached the truck, I saw Sheriff Jefferson coming towards me with a young fellow in a smart city suit who was a stranger to me.

It was too late to duck out of sight, so I waved to Jefferson, making out I was glad to see him.

'I want you to meet Matt Lawson,' he said. 'Mr Lawson, this is Terry Regan who I was telling you about.'

Lawson thrust out his hand. He looked just out of college and as bright and as sharp as they come.

I shook hands with him.

'Mr Regan,' he said, 'I understand from Sheriff Jefferson you look after all the TV sets in the district.'

'Well, I wouldn't say all of them, but I certainly look after most of them.'

Jefferson said, 'I'll leave you two gentlemen to discuss your business. I promised Doc I'd give him a game of checkers.'

He shook hands with Lawson, told me he expected me to look him up soon, and then walked over to his office.

Lawson said, 'I'll cut it short, Mr Regan, as you're in a hurry. I'm from the National Fidelity, and I'm selling TV insurance. I was wondering if you would give me a list of your clients. It would save me a lot of leg work. I don't expect you to give me the list for nothing. I suggest I pay you a quarter of my commission on any sale I make.'

Although I wasn't in the mood to talk business right then, I wasn't so stupid not to see the advantage of such a proposition.

'What kind of insurance are you selling?' I asked.

'The usual: coverage for the tube, all maintenance charges and spares. All I want is the names and addresses of people owning sets in the district.'

'Well, okay. I have my address book in the truck. I'll lend it to you. You make a copy of it and give the book to the Sheriff. I'll pick it up when next I'm in town.'

He said he would do that.

As I searched for the address book, I said, 'I didn't know the National Fidelity did TV insurance. I thought they only handled life policies.'

'We cover the whole insurance field. Of course our biggest business is in life.'

I gave him the address book and then shook hands with him and drove back to my cabin.

I had collected the various spares for Delaney's super-set, and I started work on the set during the afternoon.

I worked on it for two reasons: because I had never been given the chance to build a real super-set before, and it did my pride good to tackle such a job, but also, and much, much more important, because I knew instinctively that Gilda had meant what she had said, and this super-set would give me a legitimate excuse to go up to Blue Jay cabin and spend some time there installing the set, and while I was there I would be able to see her.

So I worked on the set, my ears cocked for the telephone bell to ring which didn't ring, waiting for her to change her mind and knowing she wouldn't change her mind, and feeling as bad as a man can feel who is fatally in love with a woman, wanting her every moment of the day and knowing he isn't going to have her.

And as I worked on the set, I became more and more aware that the one obstacle standing between Gilda and myself was an elderly man who sat day after day in a wheel chair, a helpless cripple, who was no use to himself nor to anyone else.

II

The following day I drove down to Los Angeles to select wood for the cabinet I was going to build for Delaney's super-set. I discussed with the cabinet maker how I wanted the wood cut and he promised to have it ready in an hour.

With an hour to kill, I wandered the streets, shop window gazing. I came upon a jeweller's shop, and, in the window, I saw a blue and silver powder compact. It attracted my attention because the blue in it exactly matched the colour of Gilda's eyes.

I went in and bought it.

21

I told the salesman to put Gilda's name on the inside lid and he did it while I waited.

When I got back to my cabin, I went to the telephone, picked up the receiver and called Blue Jay cabin.

The sound of her voice as she said 'Yes? Hello?' set my heart thumping.

'Will you have dinner with me in Los Angeles tomorrow night?' I said, speaking slowly and distinctly. 'I'll be outside the gate at eleven.'

There was a very slight pause, then she said, 'I'm afraid you have the wrong number. No, it's quite all right. It's no trouble,' and she hung up.

I guessed Delaney was in the room and was listening to her. I replaced the receiver.

There was nothing more now I could do except wait for tomorrow night.

At a quarter to eleven, wearing my best suit, I drove over to Blue Jay cabin.

At one minute to eleven, she came down the path.

The sight of her sent my blood racing. I stood there, my hands resting on the top of the gate, watching her as she moved towards me with that liquid grace of hers.

When she reached me, she paused and looked at me. I opened the gate and she moved through to my side.

'Hello, Terry,' she said.

That wasn't quite the greeting I had expected. There was nothing much I could say to that, but I did what I wanted to do: I grabbed at her.

I grabbed nothing. She slid away from me. It was like trying to catch hold of a shadow.

'No, Terry!'

The sharp note in her voice chilled me.

'What do you mean – no?' I said. 'I've been living for this moment ever since I called you.'

'Yes, and so have I, but I told you: we are not going to make love together again. If you can't see me without that, then we can't meet. We can't be anything to each other except friends.' 'Friends? After what you and I have been together?'

22

'All right, Terry. I'll go back. I'm sorry, but that's the way I feel. I shouldn't have come down to meet you. If we can't just be friends, then I can't see you again.'

I drew in a long, deep breath.

'Okay,' I said. 'I'll accept the terms.'

'Is it so hard for you, Terry?'

'Never mind that. You heard what I said: I accept the terms. Let's go. It's getting late.'

She walked with me to the truck and got in beside me.

'There's a restaurant I know,' I said as I started the engine. 'It's out of the way and safe. No one will know us there.'

'Thank you for thinking of that.'

It was an eighty-mile run down to Los Angeles. It was a good road, but it took the best part of two hours to get there. We didn't say much to each other during the run. She made the effort at first and prattled about this and that, but it was talk that meant nothing, and she seemed to realize it for she suddenly stopped, and the rest of the run was made in silence.

The Italian restaurant I had chosen was out at Hermosa Beach. The food was supposed to be good.

When we reached the restaurant I steered the truck into the parking lot, and we went together to the terrace overlooking the sea where there were tables with shaded lamps, and soft music that couldn't offend anyone and waiters in white coats moving about quickly and efficiently as slick as a well-oiled machine.

We had dinner of scampi, *escalope alla Bolognese* and a bottle of good red wine.

I kept looking at her, hoping to see that thing in her eyes, but it wasn't there. It was as if the lighted windows of the house that you knew always gave you a welcome were screened suddenly with black blinds.

'I'm loving this, Terry,' she said when they brought the escalopes. 'This is the first time I have been taken out for nearly four years.'

'I'm glad I got the idea,' I said. 'If you can fix it, maybe we'll come again.'

23

Probably she caught the bitter note in my voice. She looked quickly at me.

'Terry . . . tell me something about yourself. This shop of yours: are you very ambitious about it? Tell me how you feel about it.'

I wasn't interested, but if she wanted to keep up this grotesque pretence, I had to go along with her.

'Well, if I had some money,' I said, pushing the food around on my plate but not eating it, 'I'd buy myself a shop. I know just the place. This running around servicing people's sets and selling here and there won't ever get me anywhere. What I need is a shop with a good window where I can display hand-built Hi-Fi sets and sell discs in a good demonstration room. That's what I want, but getting it is not so easy. I could never dig up enough money.'

'How much would you need?' she asked, looking intently at me.

'That depends. Twenty-five thousand would take care of it. Twice that amount to do something on the grand scale.'

'If he died, Terry, you would have all the capital you need.'

'That's right,' I said. 'You told me that before. If he died ...'

I saw her glance furtively at her watch.

I beat her to it.

'You'll be wanting to get back. He might be wanting a pill or something.'

'Oh, Terry, please...'

I snapped my fingers at the waiter and got the check. As we walked back to the truck, she said, 'I've loved every second of this, Terry.'

'I'm glad.'

I wasn't going to be such a hypocrite as to say I had loved it too.

I got the truck moving, and we drove out of Los Angeles and hit the mountain road.

We didn't talk.

When we were within a couple of miles from Blue Jay cabin, I pulled up.

She turned quickly to look at me.

24

'Why are you stopping?'

'There's something I want to give you.'

I took the package containing the compact out of my pocket and dropped it into her lap.

'What is it, Terry?'

I turned on the dashboard light.

'Open it and see.'

She slipped off the elastic band, undid the wrapping and opened the box.

The compact looked terrific in its bed of cotton wool: it really looked something.

I heard her draw in her breath sharply.

'You don't really mean this is for me?'

'Yes. It matches the colour of your eyes.'

'But, Terry . . . I shouldn't accept it. You shouldn't have given it to me.'

'When I saw it I thought it looked made for you.' She touched the compact, then turned it over in her fingers. 'You are tempting me, Terry, and I can't resist it.' 'I don't mean to tempt you,' I said. 'There are no strings tied to it. I just wanted you to have it.'

I leaned forward, started the engine and drove fast to Blue Jay cabin.

She sat beside me fingering the compact and silent.

When we reached the gate and I had stopped, she got down from the truck and I joined her.

We stood looking at each other.

'You don't know how much I've enjoyed this, Terry: thank you for being so understanding, and thank you again for this lovely compact. It's my first present in years. I love it.'

She swayed towards me, her arms sliding around my neck and her mouth found mine.

There wasn't any satisfaction in it for me. As I held her, I was thinking of the man lying in his bed, probably asleep, not a hundred yards from where we stood, and I knew so long as he was alive, there was only this furtive thing that was happening now between us.

25

III

Gilda called me early the next morning.

'When I got back to the cabin,' she said, 'he was awake. The light was on in his room.'

My grip on the telephone receiver tightened.

'Did he know you had been out?'

'I don't know. He is very quiet and sulky this morning. He hasn't said more than a few words. Listen, Terry, I can't do this any more, You must keep away from me. I'm sorry, but I'm not going to see you again, Forgive me ... I was thoughtless to have started this, Please don't telephone, and please keep away from me. He must never find out, Terry, darling. I'm sorry...'

'Now, look, Gilda,' I said, 'we can't stop now...'

'He's coming...'

The line went dead.

When a man is in love with a woman as I was with Gilda I reckon he is a little out of his head. I know this much: after four days and four long, hellish nights, I was in a pretty bad way. I couldn't settle to anything. My work went haywire. I got short-tempered with my clients. I didn't sell anything.

I kept thinking of her.

I telephoned Blue Jay cabin three times: once, Maria, the fat Mexican maid, answered and I hung up. Once Delaney answered and I hung up. Once Gilda answered and she hung up.

I went out there at night and prowled around their garden like a sneak thief. Just to see her silhouette against the blind of her bedroom window made me feel so bad it scared me.

On the fifth night, I got out the whisky bottle and gave myself a shot that practically stunned me. I'm not a drinking man, but I realized I had to have something to dull this raging ache for her, and the whisky did the trick. For the first time for four nights, I slept, but I dreamed about her.

But why go on?

Eight days after we had last seen each other something happened to bring this nightmare thing to a head.

26

It was nine in the evening. There was no moon and there was a hint of rain. I was sitting on the verandah, smoking and brooding into the darkness. I was a little high, and I was set to get stinking again. I heard the telephone bell ring.

I went into the sitting-room and took up the receiver.

'Is that you, Regan?'

I recognized Delaney's voice. The sound turned me cold sober and set my heart hammering.

'Yes.'

'The set's packed up. I think the tube's gone.'

This was the first good news I had had during those long hellish days. Here, at last, was a legitimate excuse to see her again.

'I'll come over right away.'

'Tomorrow will do.'

Tomorrow was Friday. There was a chance she would be down at Glyn Camp and I would miss her.

'I can't come tomorrow,' I said. 'I'll be right over.'

'Okay: please yourself.'

I hung up.

I got to Blue Jay cabin in under ten minutes.

There was a light on in the lounge. I got off the truck, collected my kit and walked up onto the verandah.

I was pretty worked up at the thought of seeing her again, but when I walked into the lounge I found Delaney reading and alone.

I hadn't thought of that possibility. I hadn't thought she would deliberately avoid me, and it gave me a hard, jolting jar of disappointment.

Delaney waved towards the TV set.

'I guess the tube's burnt out,' he said.

As I began to check the valves, Delaney, who had been watching me, said abruptly, 'I'll give you a tip. If ever my wife offers you a ride in the car, don't accept. She's dangerous in a car. I was fool enough to let her drive me once: only once, mind you, but it was enough. I've been in this chair ever since.' I didn't say anything. After a moment or so, I found a burnt out valve.

27

I went out to the truck to get a replacement. I saw there was a light in Gilda's bedroom. The blind was down. She was in there, keeping out of sight.

I went back into the lounge and fitted the valve. Then I turned on the set. The picture came up. I adjusted the contrast, tested the sound, then turned the set off.

'It's okay now', I said.

'Well, that was simple enough,' Delaney said. 'What do I owe you?'

'Three dollars.'

Raising his voice, he shouted: 'Gilda! Come here!' The way you call to a dog when your temper's short.

It was then I noticed a half full bottle of whisky and a glass on the table near him and I realized he had been drinking heavily.

The door opened and Gilda came in. I was shocked to see how pale she was. She looked at me, her eyes screened, and she nodded politely.

'Give me three dollars,' Delaney said, snapping his fingers impatiently at her.

She crossed the room to where her bag was lying on the sideboard.

I had just fixed the back of the TV set in place. As I tightened the last screw, she walked over to Delaney and opened her bag. She took out three one-dollar bills, and as she did so, the bag slipped out of her hand. It fell on the floor and its contents spilled out by Delaney's chair.

Right where he couldn't fail to see it was the blue and silver powder compact I had given her.

Delaney stared at the compact.

For a split second Gilda seemed paralysed, then she darted forward and snatched up the compact.

Delaney grabbed her wrist, twisted it brutally, and wrenched the compact out of her hand.

She tried to get it from him.

All this happened in seconds.

His face vicious, Delaney swung his left hand and struck

her very hard across her nose and mouth. The sound of his hand hitting her made a tiny explosion in the room.

The force of the blow sent her reeling. She lost her balance and fell on her hands and knees.

I remained where I was, fighting down a murderous impulse to get my fingers around his throat and choke the life out of him.

Muttering under his breath, Delaney stared at the compact.

Gilda got unsteadily to her feet. Her nose was bleeding slightly. She looked bad, with blood running down her chin, and her face white and tense.

Delaney opened the compact and stared at her name engraved on the inside flap. Then he looked up, his face contorted with rage.

'So you've found a lover,' he said and the viciousness in his voice sickened me.

Gilda didn't say anything. She leaned against the wall, her hands pressing her breasts, blood dripping from her nose on to her dress.

'So you're not content to have made me a cripple, you have to act the whore as well.'

He threw the compact across the room. It hit the opposite wall. The lid broke off and the mirror smashed.

Gilda ran out of the room.

Delaney suddenly seemed to become aware of me.

'Get out!' he shouted. 'If you spread this over your lousy little town, I'll fix you! I'll sue you to hell! Get out!'

I picked up my tool kit and went out of the room, down the steps to the truck.

I drove to the gate, pulled up and got out to open the gate.

Gilda came out of the darkness and into the light of my headlights.

She looked bad. Her nose was bruised, and there was dried blood on her chin and her eyes were glittering.

I started towards her.

'Don't touch me!'

The hysterical note in her voice brought me to a standstill.

29

'You can't stay with him now, Gilda,' I said. 'Not after this. Come with me! I'll make you happy! He'll have to give you a divorce!'

'No! Keep away from here!' she said, the words spilling out of her mouth. 'It was because I was fool enough to fall in love with you that my life is now being threatened.'

'Don't talk like that! You can't stay with him now! You've got to come with me!'

I grabbed hold of her and tried to pull her to me but she wrenched herself free.

'Keep away from me! Do you want me to go down on my knees and beg you to keep away from me? I can persuade him that I bought that compact myself if you will only keep away from me! How many more times do I have to tell you I can never leave him?'

'Until he is dead,' I said quietly. 'That's what you said, isn't it?'

She made a desperate, impatient gesture with her hands. 'He won't die. He'll last for years. Keep away from me or you'll make me hate you as much as I love you now.' She turned and ran away into the darkness.

I didn't attempt to go after her.

This was the moment when I decided to kill him.

There was no other way out for us.

I was surprised I hadn't thought of this solution before.

Chapter III

I GOT back to my cabin, put on my pyjamas and laid down on the bed.

Murder!

I had no compunction about killing Delaney. Now that I had arrived at the solution, it was as if pressure had been removed from my mind that before had been crushing it. I felt a different being.

So I lay there and I thought about the problem: how I could kill him and get away with it.

So many men had thought as I was thinking: how they could murder someone safely, and nearly all of them had made a fatal mistake and had been caught.

There must be no mistake, I told myself. Unless I was absolutely convinced I could kill him and get away with it, I mustn't attempt it.

The advantages that went with his death were a spur to my thinking. Gilda would be free, and she would be mine. Also his money would be hers and mine too. We would be able to begin a new life together. With the money, I knew I could make a success of my life. I had the training, the craftsmanship and the knowledge, but, without any working capital, I was sunk.

If I could only think of a way to kill him safely, in a way that no one would suspect that I had done it, then a new and exciting life waited, not only for me, but for Gilda.

But it was difficult. He never went anywhere, so he would have to be killed in the cabin. It would have to be done when Gilda was down at Glyn Camp. Therefore the time was fixed and not flexible. It would have to be done on a Friday between nine-thirty, when Gilda left for her weekend shopping, and midday when she returned. It would have to be done in daylight. This alone made it difficult and dangerous. Although the road leading past Blue Jay cabin was seldom used, the odd

31

person did use it, and I might be seen going there or leaving there. I had also to think of the maid, Maria, who would be in the cabin. I had to arrange that she wasn't there when I did it.

Whatever the plan was, I had to be absolutely certain that Gilda couldn't be implicated. I myself had to have a fool-proof, cast-iron alibi in case the police found out that Gilda and I had been lovers.

I thought it was unlikely that they would find this out, but there was always a chance that someone had seen us when we had gone to the Italian restaurant at Hermosa Beach and would report to the police once the murder made headlines. This murder had to be fool-proof. There was no point in my killing him if I was to end up in the gas chamber. If I killed him, I meant to have Gilda and the money.

It seemed a hopeless problem, and, although I racked my brains half the night, no safe plan came to me.

It was Delaney himself who showed me how it could be done.

The following morning, as I was about to leave my cabin, the telephone bell rang.

I picked up the receiver.

It was Delaney.

'That you, Regan?'

I can't describe the sensation that ran through me at the sound of his voice.

'Yes,' I said.

'Will you come over?' he said. 'I have something to say to you. I would take it as a favour if you'd come.'

Into my mind came a picture of him hitting Gilda and of her sprawling on her hands and knees, blood running down her face onto the carpet.

Today was Friday. She wouldn't be there. I had an urge to look again at this man I planned to murder.

'Okay, Mr Delaney. I'll be over.'

I reached Blue Jay cabin after half-past nine.

Delaney was sitting on the verandah, a glass of whisky in his hand. His face was flushed and his eyes were over-bright.

32

'Sit down, Regan,' he said, waving to a chair near hiş. He took out a pack of cigarettes and offered me one. 'Have a smoke.'

I took the cigarette and sat down. Just to look at him: the man I was planning to murder, gave me a creepy feeling.

He leaned back in his chair.

'I want to apologize. I'm sorry about that sordid scene last night. I was drunk.' He drank some of the whisky, grimacing a little. 'It isn't exactly fun to find out that your wife is being unfaithful, and I guess I went off the deep end.'

'You don't have to excuse yourself to me. It's none of my business.'

'I wanted to say I am sorry you happened to be a witness of such a sordid scene and ask you not to talk about it.'

'I don't talk about other people's affairs, Mr Delaney,' I said. 'Is that all you want to see me about? If it is, I'll get moving. I have a lot of work to do.'

I got to my feet.

'How's that set you're making me getting on? When can I have it?'

'I'll deliver it on Monday.'

'Fine.' He lit a cigarette and then, squinting through the smoke, he said, 'What do you think of my wife, Regan?'

Did he suspect that I was her lover?

'What do you expect me to say to a question like that?' I asked, keeping my face expressionless.

'I just wanted your opinion.' He leaned back in his chair. 'I'm going to tell you something about her, then maybe you won't think I'm such a heel to have hit her.'

'I have work to do, Mr Delaney. I've got to get going.'

Delaney said, staring at me, 'I saw her for the first time in the swimming pool at the studios. She worked there at the kind of job they give girls with nice bodies and no brains. I've seen plenty of stars in that pool, but when I saw her, the sight of her took my breath away.' He emptied his glass, then refilled it, splashing whisky into it with an unsteady hand. 'I fell for her, Regan. I thought of her night and day. I propositioned her, but she wouldn't play. It was marriage or nothing. Imagine! I

33

could have fallen for all the glamour stars in the business but I was mug enough to fall for her. I fell for her because of the way she looked when she climbed out of the swimming pool with water dripping off her and her swim suit plastered to her like a second skin.'

I stood there, listening to him, wanting to get away, but his words hypnotized me the way a snake hypnotizes a rabbit.

'Do you know what the matter is with my wife?' he asked, leaning forward to stare at me. 'I'll tell you: she's mad about money. That's all she thinks about. If I hadn't any money she wouldn't stay ten minutes with me. Do you know what the first thing she wanted me to do as soon as we were married? She wanted me to take out an accident insurance policy. She got a man from an insurance company to talk to me. He tried to persuade me to take out a hundred thousand coverage. To stop her nagging me – and God! how she nagged! – I told her I had taken out the policy. She wouldn't believe me until I showed her the signed policy, but she didn't know I tore it up once she had seen it.' He showed his teeth in a bitter, snarling grin. 'Do you know what happened then? We went to a party. I got a little high and she insisted on driving. Like a fool I let her. I went to sleep. Somewhere up the mountain road she stopped, got out of the car to talk to a pal of hers who had stalled his car right across the road. She set the parking brake or at least she said she did when the police questioned her. Anyway, the car rolled down the mountain side with me in it. It's taken me a long time to figure that one out. Do you know what I think now? I think she wanted the hundred thousand dollar insurance pay-off more than she wanted me.'

'I don't want to listen to any of this,' I said. 'You're drunk. You don't know what you're saying.'

'You could be right, Regan, but it's a thought that's now going round and round in my head. Now she's found another lover I've got to watch out for myself. The man who stalled the car was a pal of hers. He could have been her lover. They could have cooked up the accident between them. There was a time the police thought so, only I was in love enough with

34

her to tell them I had touched the parking brake. I believed in her then, but not now.'

I didn't believe a word he had said, but I was glad he had sounded off. It made it that much easier for me to kill him.

'I'll get along, Mr Delaney,' I said and started to move towards the verandah steps.

'Wait a moment,' he said: 'about this set you're making for me. Can you fix me up with a remote control gadget? I want to be able to turn the set on and off without wheeling this chair up to it every time I want to use it. Isn't there some gadget I can have to operate the set from my chair?'

It was when he said that I suddenly saw in a flash how I could kill him.

A remote control unit was the answer.

All I had to do was to make the unit alive, and in his metal chair, the jolt of electricity stepped up by coming through the TV set would kill him as surely as if he were sitting in the electric chair!

I kept moving because I was scared if he saw the expression on my face he would know I was planning to kill him.

I said over my shoulder, 'Yes, I can fix that for you, Mr Delaney.'

I went straight back to my cabin to examine this idea he had given me. I was pretty sure this was the solution to the problem I had been wrestling with last night: how to kill him and get away with it.

I realized now the only safe way to kill him was to make his death look like an accident.

Death by accidental electrocution was the answer. It had to look like an accident, so Sheriff Jefferson would be the one to handle the investigation. If it looked like murder, Jefferson would have to call in the Los Angeles police, and I wasn't going to risk having those experts making an investigation.

It wouldn't be difficult to fool an old man like Jefferson, but I didn't kid myself I could fool Lieutenant John Boos of the LA Homicide Squad. I had met him once when I had worked in Los Angeles, and I knew him to be a hard, smart cop with a long string of murder arrests to his name. I had no intention of tangling with him.

The accidental electrocution idea was right, but there were some obvious snags I had to solve before I could put the plan into operation.

The first move was to complete the set I was building. So I went over to the shed I used as my workshop and started to build the set.

As I worked I thought of Gilda.

With every wire I soldered into place, with every valve I put into position, I told myself I was getting nearer to giving Gilda her freedom and beginning a new life with her.

I must have been out of my head, but that's the way a man can act when he is in love with a woman just out of his reach as I was with Gilda.

II

First thing on Monday morning, I loaded the set onto the truck and drove over to Blue Jay cabin.

I hadn't seen Gilda since Delaney had hit her, and I wasn't anxious to see her. I had thought of her ceaselessly, but I didn't want to meet her face to face until I had completed my plan. I was scared she might say something that would turn me away from the plan, and I was determined to go through with it if it was the last thing I did.

As I drove up towards the cabin, I saw her washing down the Buick.

I didn't slow down.

She glanced around, and for a brief moment our eyes met, then I was past her.

Delaney was reading the newspaper. He looked up as he heard the truck and, dropping the paper, he wheeled himself to the rail of the verandah.

'Here it is, Mr Delaney,' I said, 'as promised.'

'Nice work, Regan. What's it like?'

'You can judge that for yourself,' I said and carried the loudspeaker up the steps and into the lounge.

It took me about half an hour to install the set, then I explained to Delaney how it operated.

As soon as I put an LP record on the turntable and turned up the volume, I could see the impact the reproduction made on him was what I had been sure it would be.

'Why, it's like having a live orchestra in the room!'

What pleased him most was the remote control unit which I clipped to the arm of his chair. It was a small thing with three knobs: one to turn the set on and off, the other two to take care of the contrast and the volume.

When I had bought the control unit each knob had been heavily insulated with rubber caps. These I had removed together with the rubber backing so that its steel base now rested on the steel arm of Delaney's chair.

Finally, after he had examined everything, tested everything and watched a short film on the TV, Delaney turned the set off, using the control unit, and he looked at me, his face animated.

'Some set! It's a sale!'

'You have the best, Mr Delaney,' I said, my eyes on his hand, resting on the control unit.

Then he said something that showed me that luck was working on my side.

'You don't happen to know of a woman who would come out here and run the cabin, do you? This damned Mexican servant of ours isn't coming any more. She says it's too far for her to walk from the bus stop. She'll be leaving tomorrow.'

The Mexican maid had been one of the major snags in my plan. I couldn't have gone through with the plan that was now taking shape in my mind if there had been anyone else in the cabin at the time he died. Now the snag had suddenly ironed itself out.

'I'll ask around, Mr Delaney, and if I hear of anyone, I'll let you know.'

'Thank you and thanks again for the set. I'll send you a cheque.'

He put his fingers on the knob of the control unit and turned on the TV.

It gave me a crazy sensation to see his fingers on that

knob. If luck kept coming my way, on Friday when he did that, he would be a dead man.

I left him staring at the lighted screen and drove fast past the garage.

Gilda stood by the Buick, looking towards me. I half raised my hand, but I kept on. I didn't look at her as I passed her. In the driving mirror I could see her, staring at me, obviously startled.

I returned to my cabin.

With the maid out of the way, I had got over one of the major snags in my plan. Now if I could only be sure that Gilda went down to Glyn Camp on Friday, Delaney would be on his own.

But would he turn the set on?

I checked the week's TV programme magazine and it gave me quite a jolt to see that on Friday morning one of the channels was going to show a film of Jack Dempsey's famous fights, and it was being shown at nine forty-five a.m. I knew Delaney wouldn't miss seeing such a film. Again it looked as if luck was running my way.

But there was still the biggest snag to get over.

I would have to get into Blue Jay cabin on Thursday night to make the control unit alive. Also I had to be well away from the cabin at the time Delaney died. Suppose Gilda changed her mind about going to Glyn Camp or suppose Delaney touched the control unit before she left?

If he did that; she might find him, touch him and get killed herself. How was I to be absolutely sure Delaney would only touch the control unit at the exact time I wanted him to touch it and when he was alone?

This was a real headache.

I was still brooding about it and getting nowhere when I heard a car coming up the lane.

For a moment I thought it might be Gilda and I jumped to my feet, but it wasn't Gilda. It was Matt Lawson, the insurance salesman.

He left his car at the gate and came over to me.

'Hello there, Mr Regan,' he said in his breezy college

manner. 'I've brought you some money. It's not much, but it's better than nothing. I managed to sell twenty policies up here.'

'That's pretty good,' I said, anxious to be rid of him.

'I have the figures right here.' He gave me a statement and two ten-dollar bills. 'That covers it I think.'

I glanced at the statement, nodded and put the bills in my pocket.

'Well, thanks,' I said.

'Have you seen the new Trojan radio and TV set they're showing at the Acme Store in LA, Mr Regan? It's certainly a dandy. I didn't know if you would be interested in getting the agency for it up here.'

'I haven't seen it yet,' I said. 'I build most of my own sets, but I'll certainly take a look at it.'

'What I like about it is the time clock on it. All you have to do is to set the clock and at the right time the set switches on your programme.'

I had to make an effort not to show my excitement. He had given me the solution to my problem

A time clock! With such a clock I could control the exact time the control unit was to come alive.

When Lawson had gone, I considered the plan now as a whole.

Unless I made some stupid slip, it was fool proof.

I had to be sure Doc Mallard would be the one to examine Delaney's body after he was dead.

The local coroner, Joe Strickland, had worked with Doc now for twenty years. He was a meek little man, and he was scared of Doc. If Doc said Delaney's death was accidental, Joe Strickland would say so too.

I was relying on the inefficiency of two old men – Doc Mallard and Sheriff Jefferson – to cover up murder, and in this particular setup in this particular little town, unless I made a really glaring mistake, I was confident I would get away with it.

I now had three clear days to perfect the plan.

I had to get a time-switch clock. All the dealers in Los Angeles knew me and they might remember I had bought this article. To be absolutely safe I would have to buy it in San Francisco where I wasn't known.

The following day I drove into Los Angeles, and then took the train to San Francisco, arriving there late in the afternoon. I bought the clock. The clerk who served me practically threw it at me so anxious was he to get rid of me and the rest of the customers before closing time and I was sure he wouldn't recognize me again.

I got back to my cabin late that night.

It was then, as I lay in bed, trying to sleep, that I suddenly wondered if I had gone out of my mind to plan such a thing, but when I thought of Gilda, I got my nerve back.

Soon after eleven o'clock the following morning, I called Delaney's cabin.

As luck would have it, he answered the telephone himself.

'Regan here, Mr Delaney,' I said. 'The set going okay?'

'Terrific.'

'I don't know if you've seen the TV programme for Friday,' I said, coming to the real reason why I was calling him. 'They are showing the Dempsey fight film.'

'They are? I didn't see that. What time is it showing?'

'Nine forty-five Friday morning.'

'Well, thanks, Regan: I wouldn't have missed that for anything.'

I said I thought he would want to see it and hung up.

For some moments I stood staring at the telephone. It had been horribly easy. I had no doubt that at around nine-forty Delaney would put his hand on the remote control unit to turn on his set and at that time the unit would be lethal.

Everything now depended on whether Gilda went to Glyn Camp in the morning. That was the one thing in my plan over which I had no control.

On the mountain road, a quarter of a mile from Blue Jay cabin there was a place where I could see the cabin far below and part of the road leading to Glyn Camp. I planned to go to this place around eight-thirty in the morning and wait there.

From this vantage point I could see Gilda leave. If by twenty-past nine she hadn't left, I would drive fast to Blue Jay cabin and stop Delaney from touching the control unit. I could always cook up some excuse that I wanted to test the set and while doing so I could make the unit safe.

My next move was an easy one. I put a call through to Jeff Hamish, the writer, who had a de luxe cabin about a mile from me and about a mile and a half from Delaney's Place.

I knew Hamish was a fanatical collector of LP records and he had quite a library of them. I had picked on him to establish my alibi. He was a well-known writer and, as a witness, he would make a solid impression.

When I finally got on the telephone, I said, 'I'm sorry to disturb you, Mr Hamish, but I have a gadget here that's just made for you. It's an attachment that cleans a disc while it is playing. There's a roller dipped in a solution that keeps just ahead of the stylus and really does its job. It's just the thing for you.'

'Sounds wonderful. Let's have a look at it.'

'I'm passing your way tomorrow morning. Okay if I look in around half -past nine?'

'Sure, and thanks for remembering me,' and he hung up.

That was going to be my alibi.

Delaney would die at nine forty-five. At that time I would be demonstrating this gadget at Hamish's place, a mile and a half from Blue Jay cabin around half-past nine and ten. It was an unassailable alibi.

That was Wednesday.

On Thursday night I had the trickiest and most dangerous part of the plan to do.

A little after half-past nine, with my tool box and the time-switch clock, I started off on foot for Delaney's place.

I didn't dare risk taking the truck in case someone saw me and remembered I was heading that way at that hour.

I had a twenty-five-minute walk. I kept off the road and cut across the scrub land. There was a moon, but the night was pretty dark and I was confident no one would spot me if they happened to be on the road.

I reached the gate leading up to Delaney's cabin at ten minutes to ten.

41

Moving silently, I walked up the rough road until I came within sight of the cabin.

The light was on in the lounge and I could hear music from the TV.

I made a wide detour through the overgrown garden and came up at the back of the cabin.

I climbed the steps onto the verandah, moved to the back door and gently turned the handle. The door swung inwards, and I stepped into the kitchen.

The door was open, and the light from the hall was enough for me to see where I was going. I moved silently to the door and looked into the dimly-lit passage.

The strident sound of jazz was coming from the TV set.

Delaney had the volume well up so I had no fear of him hearing me. I went to the storeroom and eased open the door.

I had a flashlight with me and I turned the beam into the dark little room. I moved in and gently closed the door.

Well, I was in. I had a long wait ahead of me.

I cleared a space by the door so that, if Gilda happened to look in, I could hide behind the door. Then I lowered myself to the floor and rested my back against the wall.

The tension and the hell of waiting began.

It was just after half -past ten when I heard the TV set turn off. I got to my feet, and moving against the wall, I listened, my heart thumping.

I heard the sound of a door shutting.

The partition of the storeroom was thin and sounds came clearly to me.

I heard Delaney say, 'Are you going to bed?'

Gilda said, 'Yes, as soon as I have locked up.'

Then I heard the bolts of the front door being pushed to, and a moment later, I heard her come down the passage and go into the kitchen. I heard her lock the back door and shut the window.

I waited, holding my breath, wondering if she would come into the storeroom, but she didn't.

She went back into the lounge.

I heard her say 'Good night.'

'There was something I've been meaning to ask you,' Delaney said. 'What's happened to your lover? You haven't been sneaking out at night recently. I've been watching for you. Has he got tired of you already?'

'I'm going to bed. Good night.'

'I'm in the mood for some diversion tonight,' Delaney said. 'After all you divert your lover – why not your husband?'

'You're drunk,' she said, her tone contemptuous. 'You don't know what you're saying.'

I heard her move to the door, then there was a sudden scuffling noise and I heard her scream.

I jerked open the storeroom door and stepped out into the passage. From where I stood I could see into the lounge.

Delaney had caught hold of Gilda by her wrist and had dragged her close to his chair. His face was congested and his eyes vicious.

'You're forgetting I'm your husband, aren't you?' he rasped. 'You have certain duties that you seem to be forgetting. If your lover is allowed to have his fun with you, why shouldn't I also have my fun?'

'Let go of me, you beast!'

He hooked his fingers in the neck of her blouse and ripped it open, then he gave her a sudden push that sent her sprawling.

He sat in his chair and cursed her.

I stood there, sweat on my face, murder in my heart, listening and watching. If I hadn't known that by tomorrow morning he would be dead I would have walked into the lounge and beaten him to death.

Gilda got to her feet and staggered away from him, her face white and her eyes glittering.

'I've had enough of you,' she said. 'I'm going to leave you!'

'Leave me?' He laughed. 'Go ahead and see where it lands you. You won't get my money when I die. You won't get a damn thing! If you want to leave, then get out!'

She walked unsteadily to the door and I ducked back out of sight.

I heard her go into her bedroom and shut and lock the door.

43

This ugly scene had left me shaking.

After a few minutes I heard Delaney turn the light off in the lounge and trundle himself down the passage and into his room. He slammed the door viciously behind him.

After witnessing this scene I had no hesitation now in going ahead with my plan. Gilda had to be freed from this man.

It wasn't until the hands of my watch stood at two o'clock that I decided it was safe to make a move.

I had been sitting in the hot stuffy darkness now for close on four hours. I was glad at last to become active. Turning on my flashlight and picking up my tool kit, I opened the storeroom door and listened.

The cabin was silent except for the faint hum from the refrigerator in the kitchen and the ticking of a clock in the lounge.

I walked silently down the passage, and into the lounge.

Very gently, I closed the door behind me, then I crossed over to the TV set.

Working quickly, I disconnected the leads to the main and took the back panel off the set. I disconnected the remote control unit's lead from the set and reconnected the lead in such a way that the boosted current would go directly to the control knobs of the remote control unit.

I then cut the mains lead and connected the two wires to the time-switch clock. I put the clock in a space in the back of the TV set.

I carefully checked what I had done. The setup was simple enough. Until the hands of the time-switch clock reached twenty minutes to ten the mains current couldn't reach the set. At twenty minutes to ten the clock would switch on the mains current and the remote control would then become lethal. When Delaney touched the unit at that time, he would receive the full shock of the boosted current coming through the valves of the TV set.

The time-switch clock safeguarded Gilda. The remote control unit couldn't come alive until twenty minutes to ten. By that time she would be on her way to Glyn Camp. If she didn't go to Glyn Camp, I still had time to get to Blue Jay cabin and make the control unit safe.

When I was certain I had made no mistake, I put the back of the set on again.

The stage was set. The success of the plan now depended on whether Gilda left for Glyn Camp in the morning.

I collected my tools, checked once more to make sure I hadn't forgotten anything, then, moving silently, I went over to the lounge window and slipped the catch back.

I pushed open the window, climbed out into the darkness of the verandah and then gently closed the window behind me.

Chapter IV

I

AT half-past eight the following morning I called the girl at Glyn Camp who relayed my telephone messages when I was out on my rounds.

'I'll be leaving in a few minutes, Doris,' I said to her. 'My first call will be at Mr Hamish's place. I'll be there around nine-thirty. If anything comes in between then and quarter-past ten, call me there, will you?'

She said she would.

It was essential to my plan that Doris should know I was with Hamish at nine-thirty. I was pretty sure that Delaney would try to turn on the TV set before the Dempsey film began. As the time-switch clock prevented the current getting into the set, the set wouldn't work. He would think it had packed up, and he was certain to yell for me.

Doris, the telephone girl, would get the message and would pass it on to me while I was with Hamish. I would tell Hamish that Delaney wanted me to call on him. I would thus establish the reason why I had gone to Blue Jay cabin and why I

45

happened to be the first to find his body. It was essential that I should be the first there as I had to set the scene before I called Doc Mallard and the Sheriff.

I had a cold empty feeling inside me as I locked up the cabin and got into the truck.

I drove fast down the mountain road until I reached the spot where I could see Delaney's cabin in the far distance

The time was now ten minutes to nine. I lit a cigarette with hands that were far from steady, and I stared down at the distant cabin.

There was no sign of any life out there, although the garage doors stood open, which was a hopeful sign. Would Gilda go to Glyn Camp? Would I have to make a mad race down to the cabin to make the remote control unit safe? It would take me about seven minutes to reach the cabin. I could wait until twenty minutes past nine, but no longer.

The next ten minutes were the longest I have ever lived through. I sat in the truck, my hands like ice, sweat on my face and my heart thumping.

I kept looking at my watch, wondering what was happening in the cabin, wondering if Gilda was getting ready to go down to Glyn Camp or if she had decided not to go.

Then suddenly I saw Gilda moving across to the garage.

I jumped to my feet.

She was going to Glyn Camp!

After a long pause, the Buick came out of the garage and drove down the tarmac to the gate. There, I lost sight of it, but I had no doubt that she was on her way to Glyn Camp as she usually did on a Friday morning, and she wouldn't return before midday.

I looked towards the cabin. There was no sign of Delaney. I looked at my watch. The time was now a quarter-past nine. In less than half an hour, he would be dead.

On the way up to Hamish's cabin, I tried not to think of Delaney, but I kept wondering what he was doing: if he had discovered yet that his set wasn't working; if he was already talking to Doris on the telephone, telling her to get me over to his place right away.

I reached Hamish's cabin at two minutes to half-past nine.

Mrs Hamish told me to go on in. She said I would find her husband in his workroom.

I went to his workroom which was at the rear of the cabin.

Hamish, a big man with a red jovial face, was sitting on the edge of his desk, the telephone receiver against his ear.

He looked up as I came in and nodded to me.

'He's here now,' he said into the mouthpiece of the telephone. 'Hold on, will you?' To me, he said, 'Here's a call for you, Regan.'

I guessed it would be Doris, calling to say Delaney wanted me to come over and fix his set. The whole plan was working like clockwork. It was uncanny: every move was coming out right for me.

'Thanks,' I said and took the receiver from him.

'I've just got to fix something,' he said. 'I'll be right back,' and he went out of the room.

When he had gone, I said, 'Is that you, Doris?'

Then I got a shock that turned me rigid.

'Terry... it's me.'

It was Gilda!

'Gilda? Where are you?'

'I'm at your place. I found the key under the mat and I asked your girl where I could find you. She told me where you were.'

'But why are you at my place?'

'I've left him, Terry.'

I felt as if someone had slugged me under my heart.

'Left him? What do you mean? You said you would never leave him!'

'We had a horrible scene last night and another this morning. I can't face any more of it, Terry. I've left him for good. I came here to talk to you about it. I'm going to ask him for a divorce.'

I was scarcely listening. Now she had left him, there was no reason for him to die! I looked at my watch. I had two minutes to save myself from becoming a murderer!

Two minutes!

'Stay where you are, Gilda,' I said. I had difficulty in controlling my voice. 'I can't talk now. I'll be with you in an hour! Wait for me – do you understand?'

'But, Terry...'

I cut the connection, then feverishly dialled Delaney's number. My hands were slippery with sweat. I was in a hell of a state.

As I listened to the burr-buff-burr on the line I again looked at my watch.

Fifty seconds!

I sat there, the receiver against my ear, my breath fast and heavy, listening to the bell ringing and slowly realizing that I was too late.

I let the bell ring until the hands of my watch crawled to a quarter to ten; then, very slowly, I replaced the receiver and got to my feet.

By now Delaney was dead and I had killed him!

There had been no need for him to have died! Gilda had freed herself by walking out on him – just as simply as that!

Well, it was done now. I had to think of myself. Panic flickered in my mind.

I heard Hamish coming, and I made an effort and pulled myself together. I moved quickly to his radiogram and began to fix the gadget I had brought with me.

He joined me.

'If that really works,' he said, 'it's just what I have been looking for.'

I spent the next twenty minutes explaining and demonstrating how the gadget worked. I was so het up I didn't know what I was saying, but Hamish was interested enough in the demonstration not to notice anything was wrong.

'It's first rate,' he said finally. 'I'll give you a cheque right away.'

As he went to his desk I suddenly remembered that Delaney hadn't called Doris and that put me on a spot. I had to tell Hamish I was going down to Delaney's place. I had to have a reason if it came to an investigation why I happened to be the first to find his body.

Maybe Doris had forgotten to call me, although I knew this was unlikely.

'Can I use your phone?'

'Help yourself,' Hamish said as he searched in his desk drawer for his cheque book.

I called Doris.

'Has anything come in?'

'There was a lady asking for you. I gave her Mr Hamish's number, but no one else has called.'

My heart began to pound. Was it possible that Delaney hadn't tried to turn the set on before the fight film began? Was it even possible he hadn't yet touched the remote control unit and was still alive?

'Did Mr Delaney call?'

'No.'

'Okay, I'll call you later,' I said and hung up.

I was in a jam now. If Delaney was already dead, I didn't dare go to his cabin for the next hour. If he were alive, I must stop him touching the remote control unit.

I didn't hesitate. Hamish had written the cheque and had got up to examine the gadget I had fixed to the turntable. I dialled Delaney's number. After listening to the unanswered ringing for several seconds, I hung up.

He must be dead, I thought, and I felt really bad.

Fortunately for me, Hamish was trying out the gadget and wasn't paying me any attention; otherwise he would have seen the state I was in.

He waved to the cheque lying on his desk.

'There you are, Regan. You're some salesman. This is the very thing.'

'I thought of you as soon as I saw it.' I said, putting the cheque into my wallet. 'I must get down to Mr Delaney's place now. I've just built him about the best set I've ever built, and I want to make sure he is satisfied.'

'What have you given him?'

I explained the set.

I had to spin out time. I didn't dare get to Blue Jay cabin

before a quarter to eleven. By then Delaney would have been dead an hour, and that should be good enough for an alibi.

'What sort of fellow is Delaney?' Hamish asked, sitting on the edge of his desk. 'I looked in on him about a week ago, but he didn't seem to welcome me. Do you know his wife?'

'I've met her,' I said cautiously.

'Some girl!' Hamish said, admiration in his voice. 'What a body she's got! It can't be a lot of fun for her to be tied to a cripple.'

'That's a fact.' I glanced at my watch. It was twenty minutes to eleven. 'Is that the right time?' I nodded to his desk clock.

'Could be a little slow. I'd say it was close on twenty to eleven.'

'I must get going.'

'Well, thanks, Regan. If you find anything else you think I could use, let me know.'

I drove down to Blue Jay cabin at a moderate speed. My nerves were screwed up and my hands were clamped on the steering wheel in a knuckle-white grip. I kept wondering what I was going to find when I walked into the cabin. Would he be alive?

There was just the chance he had been sitting on the verandah and hadn't bothered to answer the telephone. There was just a chance he had forgotten the fight film was showing.

I did something I hadn't done for as long as I could remember. I began to pray. I prayed that when I walked into the cabin, I would find him there - alive.

II

As I stopped the truck before the gate leading up to Blue Jay cabin, the mail van came up the road and pulled up beside me.

Hank Fletcher, the Glyn Camp postman, grinned cheerfully through the open van window and waved two letters at me.

'Going up to see Mr Delaney?' he said. 'Will you save me the walk and take these letters?'

This was a stroke of luck. Here was another witness of the exact time I had arrived at Blue Jay cabin. I went over to him.

'Sure,' I said, taking the letters. I looked at my watch. 'Have you the right time on you, Hank?'

'It's five after eleven, and that's dead right.'

He waved to me and drove away down the road.

I glanced at the two letters he had given me. They were both for Delaney. I crammed them into my hip pocket, then opened the gate and drove the truck through, got out, shut the gate, then drove up to the cabin.

I was now breathing like an old man with asthma and my heart was thumping.

Was Delaney dead? I kept asking myself. Had I killed him?

I got off the truck and stood looking at the silent, deserted verandah. He wasn't there, and that looked bad. I walked slowly up the steps.

The door leading into the lounge stood open. I paused. Across the lounge I could see the screen of the TV set, like a white eye that glared at me.

I moved forward, and then stopped abruptly.

Delaney was lying on the floor, his hands hiding his face. No one could lie like that unless he was dead. There was a horrible rigidness about him that told me he must be dead.

I stood in the doorway, looking down at him, and I felt scared and sick.

I had done this thing. I had killed him.

Slowly, I moved into the lounge. I realized the danger I was now in. If I made one slip, I too would die. I had to go through with my plan. I was certain it was fool proof. All I had to do was to carry it out step by step and I must be safe.

Moving around his rigid body, I turned off the main's switch, then I disconnected the plug from the mains to the set.

I bent over him and put my fingers on the back of his neck. I had to force myself to do it, but I had to be absolutely sure he was dead. The touch of his cold skin against my hot fingers told me as nothing else could that he was dead, and he had been dead some little time.

Crossing to the door, leading onto the verandah, I shut it,

51

then I went back to the TV set, unscrewed the fastening screws and removed the back of the set.

I stripped out the time-switch clock and the wires from the remote control unit and reconnected them in their correct position.

I worked fast, and the whole job took under five minutes. Then I took the clock out to my truck and hid it under the driving seat. I got a length of flex and, returning to the lounge, I replaced the mains lead that I had cut the previous night.

I went out of the room and to the storeroom and hunted around until I found a tool box. This was on the top shelf, and I nearly missed it. In it I found two screwdrivers: one insulated and the other all steel. I took the all steel one and returned to the lounge. I placed the screwdriver on the floor close to Delaney's right hand.

Then I worked on the remote control unit. I put back the insulated rubber caps and the rubber back.

I then turned the TV set so that its open back faced Delaney's body.

I stood back and surveyed the scene.

It looked convincing enough to me except for an empty glass, lying on the carpet near Delaney. This seemed out of place. I guessed he had been drinking when he had died.

I picked up the glass. I didn't want any confusion at the inquest. It had to be kept as simple as possible. If Joe Strickland suspected that Delaney was a drunk, he might probe deeper than I wanted him to.

I took the glass into the kitchen, washed it and dried it, taking care I held it in the cloth so I wouldn't leave any fingerprints on it. I put the glass in the kitchen cupboard.

I returned to the lounge. All this had taken under ten minutes. It was time to call Sheriff Jefferson.

Before I picked up the receiver, I took one more look at the scene.

It looked convincing.

Delaney lay before the set, its back off and facing him, the screwdriver lay near his hand. Anyone coming on the scene who had no reason to doubt the setup would naturally come

52

to the conclusion that he had been electrocuted while trying to find a fault in his set.

It had often happened before. From time to time there appeared in the newspapers an account of some handyman who had tried to repair his set with the current on and had killed himself.

As I reached for the telephone, I suddenly realized that there was nothing wrong with the set! That discovery turned me cold. I had very nearly made a fatal slip. There had to be something wrong with it, otherwise why should Delaney have tried to repair it? If there was an investigation, the police would immediately become suspicious if they turned the set on and found it working properly.

I went over to the set, took from my toolbox an insulated screwdriver, turned the set on and then put the blade of the screwdriver across two terminals. There was an immediate flash from the set and a bang, blowing half the valves, and a wisp of smoke came from the set.

I disconnected the set, then I ripped loose the lead to the sound control and left it dangling. That fixed it. I went back to the telephone and called Sheriff Jefferson.

He answered at once.

'Sheriff?' I didn't have to try to make my voice sound urgent.

By now the shock was hitting me and I felt and sounded bad. 'This is Terry Regan. Will you come out to Blue Jay cabin right away? There's been an accident. Delaney's dead.'

'Okay, son.' His voice was quiet and calm. 'I'll be right out.'

'Bring Doc with you.'

'He's here. We're coming,' and he hung up.

It would take him in his old Ford the best part of half an hour to get out here.

I had a moment's breathing space and my mind went to Gilda, waiting for me in my cabin.

It was then I realized that she now had no alibi! If anything went wrong, and the police investigated, suspecting murder, they would want to know where she had been between the time he died and the time she returned to the cabin. They

53

would immediately suspect there was something between us, and that would give them the motive for the murder. I sat before the telephone, my heart thumping while my brain seized up with panic. She had been waiting at my cabin now for an hour and a half.

I would have to manufacture an alibi for her, but first I had to get her down to Glyn Camp.

I called my number. After a moment's delay, Gilda answered.

'Gilda?' I said. 'Will you please do exactly what I tell you without asking questions? This is urgent and important.' 'Why, yes, of course, Terry. Is there something wrong?' 'I want you to go down to Glyn Camp right away. Don't go by the main road; go by the lake road.' I didn't want her to run into Jefferson on his way up. 'When you get there, do your weekend shopping as usual. Don't start back until half-past twelve. Will you do that?'

'But why, Terry?, I've no shopping to do. I'm going to Los Angeles this afternoon /

'Gilda! Please! This is important! Something has happened! You've, got to do what I tell you and don't ask questions! Please do exactly what I've said! I'll meet you at a quarter to one at the cross roads on your way back and I'll explain everything. Have you your baggage with you?'

'Yes.'

'Keep it out of sight. Put it in the trunk of the car. No one must know you have left him. Will you go at once to Glyn Camp? I'll explain everything when we meet.'

'Well, all right, but I don't understand.'

'I'll see you at the cross roads at a quarter to one I said and hung up.

I went out onto the verandah and sat down. My nerves were crawling. I sat there for twenty minutes, smoking, and trying to keep my mind empty.

It was a relief when I heard the Sheriff's car come roaring up the road. Two minutes later, the battered old car pulled up outside the cabin.

Jefferson and Doc Mallard came up the steps.

'Is Mrs Delaney here?' Jefferson asked.

'No. She must be shopping in Glyn Camp. It's her day for shopping.'

'Is he dead?'

'I think so. Doc'll be able to tell us.' This was deliberate. I had now to make Doc Mallard the leading actor in this scene. 'He's in here, Doc.'

Doc Mallard looked like an old, weary stork as he came up the steps. He was wearing a gallon half at the back of his head, a black gambler's frock coat and black trousers, the ends of which were thrust into a pair of Mexican riding boots.

'Hello, son,' he said to me. 'So we have a body on our hands, huh? Well, it isn't the first, and I dare say it won't be the last. Where is he?'

'In here, Doc,' I said and led the way into the lounge. 'I found him just as he is. It looks as if he was poking around in the set, touched something and got the full shock through him. He must have been pretty careless. The screwdriver he was using wasn't insulated. I found it by his hand.'

Doc scratched the side of his jaw and eyed Delaney's body.

'I've always said these TV sets are dangerous.' He looked over at Jefferson. 'Didn't I say that, Fred? Weren't those my very words?'

'You sure did, Doc,' Jefferson said, leaning against the door post, his thumbs hooked in his gunbelt. 'Is he dead?'

Doc bent and touched Delaney's neck. As he bent, his old knees creaked.

'Sure is: as dead as a mackerel.'

'Can you say how long?'

'Three hours, could be longer, not less. Rigor's well advanced. Here, son, give me a hand with him. Help me turn him over.'

I felt pretty bad as I turned the rigid body over on its back. Delaney's face was blue-tinged and congested. His lips were off his teeth in a snarl of pain. He looked terrible.

'He's been electrocuted,' Doc said. 'No doubt about it. See that blue tinge: a sure sign.'

'Any sign of burning?' Jefferson asked.

Doc examined Delaney's hands, then shook his head.

'Nope, but that doesn't mean anything. His chair's metal. He would have received an evenly distributed shock. Well...' He straightened and pushed his hat further to the back of his head. 'You won't be wanting a p.m., Fred?' There was a slightly anxious note in his voice. I had been counting on this. I had been sure Doc wouldn't feel capable of holding a post mortem.

'If you're satisfied, Doc, I am,' Jefferson said, pulling at his moustache. 'No point in cutting the poor fellow about.' He walked over to the TV set and stared at it.

'How could it have happened, son?' he asked me.

'If you poke about in a TV set with a steel screwdriver,' I said, 'you're asking for trouble. You have only to touch something that's alive and you get it.'

'Was there something wrong with the set?'

'There's a loose lead here,' and I pointed to the lead I had ripped loose.

Both Jefferson and Doc peered short-sightedly into the set.

'How did it get loose, do you reckon?' Jefferson asked.

'It was a bad soldering job. Delaney was in a hurry to get the set and I had to work under pressure. He wanted to see the Dempsey fight film. I guess when he turned the set on, he found he couldn't get the sound. He probably thought he could fix it himself without bothering me, and this is the result.'

'He didn't call you, son?'

'No.'

'What made you come out here then?'

There was no suspicion in the old man's eyes. It was just a routine question.

'I hadn't been here to check the set since I delivered it,' I said. 'I happened to be at Mr Hamish's place, and as I was passing, I thought I'd look in to see if he was satisfied, and I found him.'

'Must have given you a shock.' Jefferson moved over to look at Delaney, 'I'll call the ambulance. We'd better get him out of here before Mrs Delaney gets back.'

56

'If you don't want me, Sheriff, suppose I go down to Glyn Camp and break the news to her?' I said.

'You do that, son. It's going to be a bad shock for her. Keep her away until the ambulance has gone. Tell her I'll be here for a while. I'd like to have a word with her. Tell her there's nothing to worry about, but there'll have to be an inquest.'

I left them: two slightly fuddled old men, happy enough to accept the setup as I had arranged it.

This lack of suspicion, this readiness to accept everything at its face value was what I had been relying on.

As I drove down to meet Gilda, I felt confident that, unless I had made a bad slip somewhere which would be discovered later, and I felt sure I hadn't, I was going to get away with murder.

III

I found Gilda waiting for me at the cross roads. She was sitting in the Buick, which she had pulled off the road onto the grass verge. Her face was pale and tense as I stopped the truck and went over to her.

'What is it, Terry?' she asked breathlessly. 'What has happened?'

'This is going to be a shock, Gilda...'

Her hands went to her breasts and her eyes turned dark with fear.

'Something's happened to Jack?'

'He's had an accident, Gilda.' I put my hand over hers. 'He's dead.'

She shut her eyes and her face went white. She remained like that for a second or so, then opening her eyes, she said unsteadily, 'Accident? What do you mean? How - how did he die?'

'He electrocuted himself. Sheriff Jefferson and Doc Mallard are up there now.'

'Electrocuted himself?' Her face showed bewilderment. 'I don't understand.'

The distant sound of an approaching siren made both of us

57

stiffen. We looked down the road. The Glyn Camp ambulance went storming past us.

I walked around the Buick, opened the off-side door and got in beside her.

'It was the TV set. A wire connecting the sound control came adrift,' I said. 'He wanted to see the Dempsey fight film. When he found he couldn't get the commentary, he must have tried to fix it himself. He touched something and got the full shock through him. In his metal chair, he didn't stand a chance.'

She suddenly began to cry, hiding her face.

I sat away from her and waited.

After a few minutes she recovered herself.

'I still don't understand,' she said, her voice shaking. 'How do you know all this? You weren't there when it happened?'

'No, of course not. I was at Mr Hamish's place. On my way down I had to pass your cabin. I went in to see if the set was working all right and I found him.'

She touched her eyes with her handkerchief as she stared at me.

'You went there when you knew I had left him and I was waiting for you?'

I had trouble in meeting her direct stare.

'I was passing,' I said rather feebly. 'After all I had sold him the set, Gilda, and he hadn't paid for it. It cost me a lot of money...'

'You walked in and found him?'

'Yes. Now listen, Gilda, they mustn't know you planned to leave him. That's why I told you to go into Glyn Camp and do your shopping as usual. You did go?'

'Yes, but, Terry, I don't understand this. Are you quite sure he was electrocuted? Did Doctor Mallard say so?' 'Yes. There's no doubt about it.'

'Then why shouldn't they know I left him?'

'There'll be an inquest. The Coroner will ask questions. If he found out you had left him, there would be gossip. This could be tricky, Gilda. You don't know what a snake-pit of gossip this place is. They might even begin to think **he killed** himself. If it was known you were at my place, waiting for me, they'd link us together, and you can imagine what they would say'

'But you said it was an accident.'

'It was an accident, but they might think he had committed suicide.'

'I think he killed himself,' she said. 'Last night we had a horrible scene, and again this morning. I told him I was going to leave him. This could be my fault. I may have driven him to it. If you bad seen his face. . . '

'Get that idea out of your mind!' I said sharply. 'It was an accident! No one would think of killing himself by fooling with a TV set.'

'But what exactly did he do?'

'He tried to get the set working again. He must have touched something and got the full shock through him. He was using a steel screwdriver and he was in that steel chair...'

'Oh, no! I'm sure it couldn't have happened like that!' She was so emphatic she began to frighten me. 'He would have to take the back off the set to touch anything dangerous, wouldn't he?'

'Yes, and that's what he did. He had taken the back off. There was this screwdriver by his hand.'

She frowned at me.

'I just can't understand it. He wasn't clever with his hands. He never has been. He never touched anything that needed repairing. He would never have thought for one moment of trying to repair the set.'

This was something I hadn't bargained for. If she came out with this information at the inquest, the Coroner might get suspicious.

'He wanted to see this film, Gilda. He was mad keen to see it.'

'How do you know he wanted to see the film?' she asked sharply.

For a moment my mind floundered, then I said, 'A couple of days ago, he called me. He wanted to know how to adjust the set. I told him about the film. He said he wouldn't miss seeing

59

it for anything. You know how fanatical he was about a fight. I'm sure when he found he couldn't get the commentary, he took the back off the set and, in trying to fix the lead, he killed himself.'

There was a look of complete unbelief in her eyes as she shrugged her shoulders wearily and asked, 'Did you say there was a screwdriver by his side?'

I began to sweat. I remembered with a real stab of fear that the toolbox had been on the top shelf in the storeroom, and this shelf had been a good seven feet from the ground. I had had to stretch up to get it. I realized now that Delaney, unable to move from his chair, could never have got near it. This was a slip, and a bad one.

'That's right,' I said.

'But he didn't know where the toolbox was kept. He never used tools.'

By now I had managed to get my second wind and I had fought down my rising panic.

'Gilda, don't try to make a mystery of this! The set broke down. He wanted to repair it. He hunted for the toolbox and he found it. He even hooked the box down with a stick. I found the box on the floor. You're trying to make this thing complicated. It happens every month. You have only to read the papers to see that people kill themselves because they are stupid enough to fool with the works of a radio or TV set. Anyone without knowledge of how a set works can kill himself . . . ' My voice trailed off when I saw she wasn't listening, and then I really began to get scared. What was she thinking? Did she suspect I had killed him?

'But it's not as easy as that,' she said, her voice shaking. 'We had this horrible, sordid quarrel. I told him I was leaving him. He never thought I would do such a thing. He was desperate and upset. He begged me to stay, but I couldn't; not after what he had tried to do to me. I am sure he wouldn't have wanted to see this fight film, not immediately after I had walked out on him. I feel sure he deliberately killed himself.'

'You're wrong! No one could kill himself like that,' I said.

This was getting dangerous. If I couldn't convince her and

she told the Coroner she suspected Delaney had committed suicide, and it got into the papers, the Los Angeles police were certain to investigate. Suicide by electrocuting oneself by a TV set was more than suspicious. 'He had been drinking. I found whisky and a glass by him. Okay, he was desperate and upset as you say. He turned the set on to take his mind off you. Finding it didn't work, he got into a rage and got hold of this screwdriver and shoved it into the works. It's just the sort of thing an unhappy, drunken man might do.'

She lifted her shoulders helplessly.

'I can't believe he would do such a thing.'

'It's got to be an accident, Gilda!' I said, my voice rising. 'If you tell the Coroner you think he killed himself, the newspapers will get it, and then you and I will be in the middle of a scandal, and that could ruin our lives.'

'Well, all right, Terry.' She suddenly seemed to relax as if the whole thing was now too much for her. 'It makes no sense to me, but I don't suppose it matters. It's so hard to believe he really is dead and at last I am free.'

I began to breathe more easily.

'We haven't much time, Gilda,' I said. 'We have to be careful. What I am going to say to you now may sound a little crazy, but it's really sound common sense. There could be an investigation. It's absolutely essential that no one knows that you and I have been lovers. If ever that gets out, we'll be in bad trouble. If they don't think he died accidentally, the Los Angeles police might poke their noses in, and they might want to know where you were when he died. You can see it would be fatal to tell them you were at my place. You must tell them you left him at the usual time to go to Glyn Camp at nine o'clock. You drove down to Glyn Camp by the lake road. On the way down you had a blow-out. It took you a long time to change the tyre. You had never done it before, and on that lonely road there was no one to help you. You didn't reach Glyn Camp until just after half-past eleven.'

I saw her stiffen and she stared uneasily at me.

'But I can't say that - it's not true!'

'You don't have to tell them anything unless they ask you,

61

Gilda,' I said, trying to keep my voice under control. 'But if they do ask you, that's the story you have got to tell them, and I mean that! If you don't, both of us could be in serious trouble. I'm going to fix your spare tyre so if they check they'll see you did have a flat.'

'Terry!' She turned and gripped my arm, staring at me, her eyes a little wild. 'You're frightening me! You make it sound as if I've done something wrong!'

'Not only you, but me as well! We have done something wrong! We have been lovers, Gilda! Don't you realize people have sympathy for a cripple? If it ever got out that we were lovers before he died, do you think they would have any sympathy for us? We would get smeared across the front pages of all the local papers. I'm trying to protect you, Gilda! You must do what I say!'

She lifted her shoulders.

'Well, all right,' she said. 'I can't think properly now, but I'll do what you say, Terry.'

I got out of the Buick, went around to the trunk, opened it and checked the spare tyre. It had been used and the tread was worn.

I went to my truck, got a nail from my tool kit and a hammer and returning to the Buick I drove the nail deep into the spare tyre. The air began to hiss out and I shut the trunk, tossed the hammer back in my toolbox and then came over to Gilda.

'You'd better get back now,' I said. 'You understand what you have to say if they ask you?'

'Yes, of course, Terry, but I don't like it. It frightens me. Are you sure I must lie about this thing?'

'Gilda, please! I wouldn't ask you if I wasn't sure you had to do it. Now one more thing: from now on until the inquest, we must be careful to keep away from each other. After the inquest, you had better go to Los Angeles. Get a room there. I'll be able to see you there. Then in a couple of months or so, we'll get married. We'll leave this district. You'll have his money, and we can have our shop.' I put my hand on hers.

'You're free now. In a little while we'll be together.'

'Yes.'

We heard a car coming down the road, and a moment later, the ambulance went past, heading towards Glyn Camp.

We looked at each other. Gilda had turned white. I felt bad myself. We both knew what was in the ambulance.

'Go on up there, Gilda,' I said. 'Jefferson is waiting for you. Don't worry. Once the inquest is over we'll be together for always.'

At that moment I really believed that, but always is a long time.

Chapter V

I

I DIDN'T get back to my cabin until late in the afternoon.

I sat on the verandah, a glass of whisky in my hand, and thought about what had happened since I had left the cabin at eight-thirty this morning.

I had killed a man. Although I could tell myself that I had dreamed up a foolproof plan and I was going to get away with it, at the back of my mind, I knew I would be wondering, during the years ahead of me, if I had made a slip that would eventually give me away.

The sound of an approaching car interrupted my thoughts.

I went to the door, my heart thumping.

Sheriff Jefferson drove in through the open gateway and, getting out of his car, he came over to me.

'I guess you could use a drink,' I said.

'Yep: I could. This has been a pretty hard day,' he said, and together we crossed the garden to my cabin. 'I've been fixing the inquest. Joe is starting his vacation the day after tomorrow, so we've had to hurry it up. We're holding it tomorrow. You'll have to give evidence, son.'

'That's okay. It's all straightforward, isn't it?' I asked as I waved him to an armchair.

'I guess so.' He sat down. He looked tired and worried.

I made two whiskies and gave him one.

He asked, 'Did you find Mrs Delaney in Glyn Camp?'

'I met her on her way back.'

Jefferson frowned, pulling at his moustache. I had a sudden uneasy feeling that he had something on his mind.

'I want to get the facts straight,' he said. 'Doc is satisfied it was an accident. What do you think?'

A cold prickle of fear began to creep up my spine.

'It couldn't be anything else,' I said, and to avoid meeting his eyes, I opened my desk drawer and took out a pack of cigarettes.

'It's a bad thing to jump to conclusions,' Jefferson said. 'The book says when a man dies you've got to consider four things: if he died from natural causes, an accident, suicide or murder.'

'It was obviously an accident,' I said.

'Yep: it certainly looks that way, but it could have been suicide.'

'You don't imagine a man would kill himself by poking a screwdriver into the works of a TV set, do you?'

'It's unlikely, son, but when a fellow's mind is upset, you don't know what he might do,' Jefferson said slowly. I'm getting old. I don't want to make a mistake now. I've been in office close on fifty years. I reckon to give up next year. The L.A. police have their knife into me. They think I'm too old to handle my job. I have only to make one mistake, and there'll be a yell of "I told you so". I want to avoid that if I can.'

'I don't see what's worrying you.'

'I thought it was an accident until . . .' He paused, frowning, then pulled out his pipe and began to load it.

I watched him, feeling suddenly short of breath.

'Until what?' I asked in a hard, tight voice.

'Mrs Delaney was planning to leave him.'

I don't know how I kept my face expressionless, but I did.

'Leaving him? How do you know?'

'I'm a meddlesome old cuss. While I was waiting for the

ambulance I took a look around the cabin. Mrs Delaney had taken all her clothes. I reckon when she left this morning, she planned not to come back.'

This was– completely unexpected, and for a long moment I sat staring at him.

'Look, Sheriff,' I said, 'does it matter whether he killed himself or whether he died accidentally? Why complicate things? If he did kill himself, and I am quite sure he didn't, it'll make things bad for Mrs Delaney. You can imagine how people will talk. Why make it hard for her?'

Jefferson continued to puff at his pipe, his expression uneasy.

'I know all that, son, but it's my duty to keep the record straight. How did she get that bruised face? It looks to me as if someone gave her a pretty hard slap and that someone could only have been her husband. That tells me they didn't get on together. That's something that should be checked. Boos would check it fast enough.'

'To hell with him!' I said. 'You're in charge up here. I think you're making too much of this. Do you really imagine any man would kill himself by poking a screwdriver into the works of a TV set? I am as sure as Doc is: it was an accident.' Jefferson shrugged.

'You could be right, son.'

'Is Doc holding a post mortem?'

'No. Between you and me, he's got beyond holding a p.m. But that doesn't matter. Anyone can see how the poor fellow died. It's why he died that bothers me.'

'Forget it,' I said. 'It certainly don't bother me.' He thought for a moment, then nodded.

'I guess you're right. I like the girl. As you say, there's no point in making it hard for her. If she did leave him, she changed her mind. That's in her favour. She was coming back, wasn't she?'

'I met her at the cross roads. She was certainly coming back.'

'Well, then...' He looked relieved. 'He couldn't have been

65

easy to live with. Maybe she got nerves. Women get nerves pretty easily.'

He finished his drink and sat for a moment staring at the floor, then he got to his feet. 'I guess I'll be moving.' He looked tired and very old. 'You'll be down for the inquest, son? It's at eleven o'clock.'

'I'll be there.'

We walked out into the evening sunlight and we paused by his old Ford.

'What's going to happen to her, do you know?' he asked.

I shook my head.

'Did he leave her much?'

'I don't know that either, Sheriff.'

I thought of the hundred and fifty thousand she told me he had. She was fixed all right, and so was I, but I wasn't going to tell him that.

'Well, I'll get along.'

I watched him drive away, then I walked back to my cabin.

I had an urge to call Gilda, but I knew it would be unsafe. I wondered what she was doing and thinking. She had the night before her alone, and so had I.

The thought of the coming night bothered me.

When fear is nibbling at you, the coming of the night with its darkness, its silence and its loneliness can be a frightening thing.

And because I had Delaney's death on my conscience, I was frightened.

II

The inquest was held in the Glyn Camp recreation hall. There were only a dozen or so people sitting on the public benches, and they had drifted in because they had nothing better to do. Delaney hadn't been known in Glyn Camp and there was no interest in his death.

I walked into the hall at five minutes to eleven. A minute later, Gilda came in. With her was a well-dressed, youngish man I had never seen before.

She came over to me and introduced the man to me. He was George Macklin, Delaney's attorney, who had come up from Los Angeles.

Macklin was around thirty-eight: a short, compact man with a lean, alert face and shrewd dark eyes.

As he shook hands with me, he said, 'This shouldn't take long. I've talked to the Coroner. He's not going to call Mrs Delaney.'

This was good news. I had been scared that Stringer might have questioned Gilda, and she might have given something away.

At eleven o'clock, Sheriff Jefferson and Doc Mallard came in. They shook hands with Gilda, nodded to Macklin and to me and sat down.

Joe Stringer, the Coroner, came in and sat behind the table in the middle of the room.

Stringer was a fat little man, nudging seventy, full of importance and without much intelligence. He opened the proceedings, and then Sheriff Jefferson gave evidence of how he had found Delaney lying before the TV set, dead.

He told Stringer that he was satisfied that there was no suspicion of foul play and that Doc Mallard would confirm this. Stringer then called Doc Mallard.

. Doc sat in the witness chair and enjoyed himself.

He said Delaney had died from a severe electric shock, and he was satisfied that the cause of death was an accident.

He pointed out that Delaney had been in an all-steel chair and had used an all-steel screwdriver. Under these circumstances, he went on, if the screwdriver came into contact with a live terminal or wire, the shock would be great enough to kill the healthiest man.

Joe chewed his pen, looked wise and made a few notes. He thanked Doc and then called me.

His first words to me told me I was three-quarters home.

'Would you tell us, Mr Regan, how the accident could have happened?'

Already he was talking of an accident. It now depended on what I said to tip the scales.

I went over to Stringer's desk and drew him a plan of the set, explaining to him how the sound control lead had come adrift, and how it was possible to get a shock by poking an uninsulated screwdriver into the set, touching one terminal, and then another. I also explained how anxious Delaney had been to see the Dempsey fight film.

'It's happening all the time, Mr Coroner,' I concluded. 'People just don't realize the danger when they fool around with a TV set when the current's going through it. The fact that he was in an all-metal chair, and using a screwdriver that wasn't insulated, didn't give him a chance.'

The blueprint I had drawn clinched it. It was something Stringer could look at and understand. I could see he was convinced as he thanked me for making it so clear, and when I got back to my seat, he looked over at George Macklin and asked him if he wanted to say anything. Macklin said he didn't, and that fixed it.

Stringer said he found Delaney had died through an unfortunate accident and he had no hesitation in recording a verdict of accidental death.

After he had gone through a long harangue about the dangers of ignorant people meddling with TV and radio sets, he left his table and came over to Gilda and offered her his condolences.

Sheriff Jefferson, Doc Mallard, Macklin and I followed Gilda out of the hall and we all paused outside in the hot sunshine.

'If there's anything I can do, Mrs Delaney,' Jefferson said, 'just let me know. I'll be happy to do it.'

Gilda thanked him. She said Macklin would take care of everything.

Macklin told her he would be out at Blue Jay cabin the following afternoon, and he would let her know how the financial situation was by then. He shook hands with her and with me, and then he, Jefferson and Doc Mallard went off together.

That left Gilda and me alone.

I was feeling fine now. Fear had left me. It had come out just the way I had planned it to come out.

'We're nearly through,' I said. 'It went off better than I thought it would. Is there anything I can do? Anything I can take care of for you?'

'There's the TV set, Terry. He – he never paid for it, did he? I wish you would take it away.'

'That's okay,' I said. 'I'll come out and take it away the day after tomorrow. Nothing else?'

She shook her head.

'Mr Macklin will take care of everything.'

Neither of us looked at each other as we talked. I was aware that we were in the main street and I was nervous people might be curious about us.

'What do you plan to do now, Gilda?'

'I don't know. It's what you plan to do. You tell me.' 'We'll have to keep away from each other for a month. I think you had better go to a hotel in Los Angeles. At the end of a month, I'll have cleared up my business here, then I'll join you. We'll go somewhere – New York or somewhere, and make a fresh start. I'll open this shop. When you are fixed up in Los Angeles, write to me. Don't telephone.'

'Then I'll see you the day after tomorrow.'

'Yes, We'll talk more then.'

I watched her walk over to where she had parked the Buick, then I started across the street to where I had left my truck. I hated her going back to the cabin on her own, but I knew I couldn't afford to take any risks of starting gossip.

It was hot, and I took my handkerchief out to wipe my face and I felt some papers in my pocket. I pulled out the two letters Hank Fletcher had given me for Delaney and I stared blankly at them. I had forgotten about them.

Gilda was getting into the Buick. I ran over to her.

'I forgot to give you these letters,' I said. 'They were delivered yesterday.'

She glanced at them, then pushed them into her bag.

'Thank you.'

We looked at each other. Those forget-me-not blue eyes were clouded and expressionless. They worried me a little.

I watched her drive away.

69

After all, a month wasn't all that long to wait, and then a new and exciting life was ahead of us.

III

I went out to Blue Jay cabin, as I had promised, to collect the TV set.

As I got off the truck, Gilda came out onto the verandah. She was wearing her cowboy shirt and jeans. She looked pale, and there were smudges under her eyes as if she hadn't slept much during the night.

'Gilda!'

I ran up the steps and took her in my arms. Her hands pressed against my chest, keeping me away from her.

'Not here, Terry!'

From the way she looked at me, I knew something was wrong. I let go of her.

'What is it, Gilda?'

She moved away from me and sat down.

'I want to talk to you.'

I sat down. I was suddenly frightened.

'Terry ... I have some bad news.'

'Well, all right.' My voice sounded husky. 'What is it?'

'There's no money.'

I stared at her. That was the last thing I expected to hear.

'No money?'

'Mr Macklin was here yesterday. He thought I knew. Jack had been spending his money recklessly ever since he was crippled. Mr Macklin kept warning him, but he wouldn't listen. The rent of this place was ridiculous. It seems he never had very much, although he told me he had. I can't think why. The money he left won't even cover his debts. I'm sorry, Terry, but there it is.'

It was a pretty hard jolt. I had been counting on Delaney's money to make a fresh start.

70

'I want you to understand, Terry,' she went on quietly, 'that I don't expect you to marry me now. I have nothing to offer you. I realize you wouldn't want to be hampered by a wife unless you had capital to make a fresh start. I think it would be better to forget about me.'

'Oh, no,' I said. 'Now look, Gilda, I love you. We can fix something. I want to marry you, and I'm going to marry you. It means we'll have to wait a little longer, that's all. We can't get married here. There would be too much talk and gossip. It'll mean I'll have to work for a firm again. I don't mind that, but we may have a tough time to start with. If you can stand it, I can.'

She hunched her shoulders, frowning.

'You don't have to do this, Terry. I can look after myself.' I got up and knelt at her side, taking her hands in mine.

'I want you, darling. Maybe it's better this way. It bothered me, thinking I would use his money. If you'll take a chance with me, I'll make good.'

She began to cry, turning her head away from me.

It was a let-down all right, but at least I had her, and she had been the real reason why I had killed Delaney.

When she had got over her crying jag and had calmed down, she said: 'I keep wondering if he killed himself. I keep wondering if it was an accident. Do you think he deliberately did this thing to provide for his debts?'

I was only half listening to what she was saying, but her last words registered and I looked sharply at her.

'Provide for his debts - what do you mean?'

'There's this insurance policy he took out.'

I stiffened. My heart began to thump.

'Insurance policy? What policy?'

'I haven't had time to tell you. He was insured. Mr Macklin told me yesterday. I didn't know myself. One of the letters you gave me was the policy from the Insurance people. He had insured the TV set. Mr Macklin says there's a clause in the policy that covers the owner of the set against an accident. He says he is sure he can collect on the policy. It'll be worth five

71

thousand dollars. It'll clear Jack's debts and give me a little something in hand until I find a job.'

If she had struck me in the face I couldn't have been more taken aback. I felt my heart turn over and my stomach muscles cramp up.

'I didn't know he had insured the set,' I said and my voice sounded far away.

'After you delivered the set,' Gilda said, 'a young man called on us. I think he said his name was Lawson. He saw the set and persuaded Jack to insure it.'

I remembered then that Delaney's name had been on the list I had lent Lawson.

'But that was only for the set. Your husband wasn't insured against an accident, was he?'

'Yes, apparently. That's what Mr Macklin tells me. He says the owner of the set is covered against an accident.'

I felt suddenly as cold as ice.

'For five thousand dollars?'

'Yes.'

My whole world began to crumble. Fear took hold of me in a grip that paralysed.

This would mean an investigation. I knew enough about insurance companies to be sure they wouldn't accept Delaney's death the way Jefferson and Doc Mallard had accepted it. They wouldn't part with a dime let alone five thousand dollars without making absolutely sure they had to pay out.

My plan and my life could now be in jeopardy because of this unexpected policy.

'There could be an investigation, Gilda,' I said. 'Is it worth bothering about? Perhaps it would be better not to put in the claim.'

She looked sharply at me.

'But it's five thousand dollars! There are bills due for three thousand. Of course I must claim.'

'These insurance detectives probe pretty deep,' I said, trying not to let her see how scared I was. 'They might easily find out about you and me, Gilda.'

'How can they? All they will want is the record of the

inquest and the death certificate. That's what Mr Macklin says.
They can't avoid paying up.'

'Don't be too sure about that. I've heard what some of
these insurance companies are like. They'll use any excuse not
to pay out. They might even try to prove he did commit suicide.
They wouldn't have to pay out then. All they would need is
one good reason to show he had killed himself, and they
couldn't have a better one if they found out he had no money
and you and I were lovers and you were leaving him.'

'You're exaggerating!'

'I'm not!' I couldn't keep my voice down. '.If they get the
slightest suspicion that you and I had been lovers, they'd tear
into us like a pack of wolves! Make no mistake about that! I'm
not saying they'd get away with it, but they could force you
to fight the claim in court. They'd stick some smart attorney
onto you who'd worm the whole story out of you, and they'd
get me in court too. We'd be smeared across the front page of
every newspaper in the district, and we'd be cooked!'

She was looking at me now as if she thought I was crazy.

'You're frightening me. What is it? Do you know more about
this thing than you've told me?'

'Of course not. I'm just warning you what could happen.
Can't we stop this claim?'

'I can ask Mr Macklin. I think it's already gone through. He
said he would deal with it as soon as he got back to his office.
Do you want me to telephone him?'

I hesitated. If Macklin had lodged the claim it would be fatal
to attempt to cancel it. It would bring the spotlight of suspicion
right on us.

'No,' I said. 'Let it go. Perhaps it doesn't matter. Perhaps as
you say, they won't make trouble.'

'Are you sure you have told me everything you know about
Jack's death?' she asked. 'You're worrying me. You make me
feel somehow guilty.'

'To the people living around here, you and I are guilty,' I
said, not looking at her. 'We're guilty of loving each other. Now
look, Gilda, I must keep away from you until this claim is
settled. There can be no question of us meeting in Los Angeles

now. Do you understand? The chances are once the claim is lodged their detectives will watch you. If they see us together, they could easily jump to conclusions.'

'But, darling, I really don't understand this,' Gilda said, a note of impatience in her voice. 'What have we got to be afraid of?'

'I'm trying to save you getting your name in the papers. This insurance company could use our love for each other to contest the claim.'

She spread her hands helplessly.

'Well, all right. I can't believe it, but if you feel that way, there's nothing I can do about it. You don't want to come near me until after the claim is settled, is that it?'

'Yes. I'm sorry, Gilda, but it is important.' I got to my feet. 'You may not think so now, but if these people find out about us, you'll realize fast enough I've been talking sense.' I moved away from her. 'I'd better collect the set and get away from here. Someone might come and find us here together.'

'Mr Macklin said the set was to be left until the insurance people had examined it.'

That gave me another bad jolt.

'Yes - I was forgetting. Well, all right. Now, look, Gilda, as soon as you have found a hotel in Los Angeles, write to me. I don't trust the girl on the switchboard. She's always listening in. I'll keep in touch with you by letter, but we must keep clear of each other.'

'All right, Terry.'

I said good-bye to her. I was so scared I forgot to kiss her.

Chapter VI

NOTHING happened for four days.

The days weren't so bad because I was busy, but the nights were really something.

On the fifth morning I got a letter from Gilda.

She was now in Los Angeles, she wrote, staying in a rooming house, and she was looking for a job without success so far. She said the insurance company was in contact with Macklin and they were sending out a representative to look at the set. The representative would arrive on Saturday morning – that was tomorrow – and would I be at Blue Jay cabin at eleven o'clock to show him the set? She said she had left the key of the cabin under the mat.

I was at Blue Jay cabin the following morning at eleven sharp.

A couple of minutes later, I heard a car coming, and I went out onto the verandah. My heart was thumping uneasily, the back of my mouth was dry and I had a cold empty sensation in my stomach.

A sleek Packard convertible drifted up the drive and came to rest by my truck.

At the wheel was a broad-shouldered, dark man around thirty-two or three with a deeply tanned, ugly but humorous face. He got out of the car as if the effect was too much for him. He sauntered up the verandah steps.

'Are you Mr Regan?'

'Yes.'

He held out his hand.

'Glad to know you, Mr Regan. I'm Steve Harmas of the National Fidelity. You know about this business?

Mrs. Delaney's attorney said you would show me the set that caused the accident.'

Well, at least he was calling it an accident. I led him into the lounge.

'That's it,' I said, nodding to where the set stood.

He glanced at the set indifferently, then sat down, waving me to a chair.

'This claim has caused a lot of writhing in our snake-pit,' he said. 'There's an uproar going on that you could hear from here if you listened that carefully.'

I said, 'Why? What's the uproar about?'

'Our claims department is run by a guy named Maddox,' Harmas said. 'He has a hornet in his chapeau. Whenever a claim comes in, he examines it the way you would examine an egg that has been laid a couple of years ago. He doesn't even wait to break the shell to be convinced it's bad. Every claim we get is treated the same way. During the year, we have something like twenty to thirty thousand claims. Two per cent, probably less, are wrong 'uns, and Maddox has found them to be wrong long before any of our super dicks have had a chance to investigate. He works by instinct, and up to now he's been right every time.' He looked sleepily at me and grinned. 'Come the day when he's wrong! Boy! Won't I cram it down his throat!'

I sat there, listening, keeping my face expressionless.

'This claim,' Harmas went on. 'Maddox thinks it's a wrong 'un. I have orders to check on it.'

'What's wrong with the claim then?' I asked.

'The way Maddox figures it is this: since we started to sell coverage for TV sets we have issued some twenty thousand policies. Our records show that during that period we have never had to pay out on the personal accident clause.' He grinned. 'Between you and me, the boys who work out the risks on this particular coverage have put that clause in about personal risk to catch a sale. We don't reckon to pay out on it.'

'It looks as if you'll have to pay out on this one,' I said.

He shrugged his shoulders.

'You could be right. All the same, I can see it from Maddox's angle. Suddenly we have a twenty-thousand to one chance dropped in our laps. That would be all right if the other circumstances are normal, but they aren't. The policy is only five days old, and the guy who took it out is buried before the policy is even delivered, and he's buried without a post mortem. Well, that would make even a mad insurance agent point like a gun dog. What it did to Maddox was nobody's business.'

'Putting it that way, it doesn't sound all that on the level,'
I said.

Harmas laughed.

'According to Maddox that would be one of the world's
great understatements. You should have heard him on the
telephone. Boy! Did he burn up that wire!' He got to his feet
and went over to the set. He opened the cabinet and peered
at the tape recorder and the turntable.

'Some set. You certainly know your business, Mr Regan.'

I didn't say anything.

'You were the one who found the body?'

'That's right.'

'Yeah. I read the coroner's report. The sound control lead
came adrift and Delaney tried to fix it and touched two
terminals and that was that. Check?'

'That's how it happened.'

He squatted down on his heels and peered into the works
of the set.

'Which terminals did he touch?'

I joined him and showed him the terminals.

'He worked with an uninsulated screwdriver?'

'Yes. I found it by his side.'

Harmas straightened up.

'He was paralysed from the waist down? That's right, isn't
it? He went around in that wheel chair?' and he jerked his
thumb to where the wheel chair stood.

'Yes'.

'Pretty rough on his wife. From what I hear, she's quite a
dish.' He made curves with his hands. 'All the right things in
the right places.'

I didn't say anything, but I was very alert now.

'You've met her?' he went on.

'Yes.'

'Would you say they got on well together?'

'What's that to do with this setup?' I couldn't keep the
irritation out of my voice. 'I have a whale of a lot to do. Mrs
Delaney asked me to show you the set. Well, you've seen it.
I've got to get going.'

77

He went back to the lounging chair and sank into it.

'Take it easy,' he said. 'I don't expect you to waste your time listening to my hot air for nothing. You built this set and you found the guy and you know the background of the district. What do you say if we pay you ten bucks a day as a retainer for technical advice?'

I hesitated, but I realized if I refused, he might get someone else. Whereas if I agreed, I'd be right in on the investigation and I could watch which way it was going.

'Fair enough,' I said. 'Ten bucks a day then.'

He took out two tens, screwed them into a ball and flicked them into my lap.

'Would you know if they got on well together?' he repeated.

'As far as I know they got on all right,' I said, 'but I didn't see much of them together.'

I wondered if he would ever find out that I had taken Gilda to the Italian restaurant. With any luck, he wouldn't dig that deep.

He stared at the TV set for a long moment, frowning, then he said, 'Do me a favour. Put the back on the set.'

'Why, sure.'

I went over to the set and put the back on, fixing the screws and tightening them.

Harmas watched me, frowning.

'Would you sit in the wheelchair?'

I stiffened, my heart beginning to thump.

'What's the idea?'

'I'm a lazy cuss,' he said, grinning. 'When I can pay a guy to do my work for me, I always reckon it's money worth spent.'

I went over to the wheelchair and sat in it. It gave me a creepy feeling, knowing Delaney had spent four years of his life in this chair.

'Will you wheel yourself up to the set and take the back off, remaining in the chair the way Delaney would have had to remain in it?'

It wasn't until I had taken out the two top fixing screws that the nickel dropped.

Seated as I was, I suddenly saw it was impossible for me to reach the two bottom screws!

As I couldn't reach these two screws, it followed that it would have been impossible for Delaney to have removed the back of the set.

If he hadn't removed the back of the set, he could not have electrocuted himself!

Here was my fatal slip!

My perfect murder plan had blown up in my face!

II

For a long, agonizing moment, I sat motionless, staring at the bottom screws. I knew Harmas was watching me. I realized he had been smart enough to have seen the screws were out of reach of anyone sitting in that big wheeled chair.

I had to do something.

I edged myself forward, and, by getting my feet off the footrest of the chair, onto the floor, I could just reach the screws by bending right forward. As I began to undo them, Harmas said sharply,' Hold it!'

The note in his voice sent a chill crawling up my spine, but I had myself under control. I looked over my shoulder at him.

He was on his feet and he was staring at the set.

'This is interesting,' he said. 'Delaney was paralysed from the waist down. He couldn't have reached those two screws.'

'Why not?'

'Look at the way you're sitting. A paralysed man couldn't sit like that.'

'He must have done,' I said, my voice was husky.

I was cursing myself for being such a fool as to put the lower two fixing screws in such a position, and not realizing that Delaney couldn't have reached them. When I had taken the back off the set I had squatted down in front of the set: the only practical way of getting at the screws.

'Well, if he did take them out, he must have had arms like a gorilla,' Harmas said. 'Here, let me have a try. Let me sit in the chair.'

I got up and stood back and watched him sit in the chair

and try to reach the screws. It was only when he was right on the edge of the chair, his feet off the foot rest and leaning well forward that he could get at them.

He sat in the chair, brooding for some moments, then he said, 'If I remember rightly, Delaney got the screwdriver from a storeroom somewhere. Do you know where the storeroom is?'

'Down the passage: first door on the right.'

'Let's take a look.'

Remaining in the chair, he propelled himself out of the lounge, down the passage to the storeroom door. He opened the door and manoeuvred himself and the chair inside.

I stood watching him, thinking what a stupid fool I had been to imagine I had dreamed up the perfect murder plan!

'Where's the toolbox kept?'

'Up on the top shelf. Delaney hooked it down with a walking stick. I found the tools on the floor.'

'Where's the stick?'

I gave him the stick with its hooked handle.

He reached up, got the hook over the side of the toolbox and tipped the box off the shelf. It came down with a clatter, spilling the tools all over the floor.

He leaned forward to pick up the screwdriver, but he wasn't within reaching distance of it. The chair, with its high wheels, made it impossible for him to pick up the tool.

He looked at me.

'You know this guy must have had indiarubber arms.'

I didn't say anything. I couldn't. To cover up, I lit a cigarette. I waited for his next move.

He got out of the chair and pushed it back into the lounge, humming gently under his breath.

I followed him and I felt pretty bad.

He sat down in one of the lounging chairs.

'I'd like to get the scene fixed in my mind,' he said. 'You found him. When you walked into the room – what did you see?'

'The chair was within a few feet of the TV set and he was lying face down on the floor in front of the set. There was this screwdriver by his hand.'

'So he had fallen out of the chair onto the floor?'

'Yes.'

'What did you do?'

'I saw the back was off the set, and I realized he had electrocuted himself. I pulled the mains plug out and then examined him to see if there was anything I could do to help him, but he was dead.'

'How did you know that?'

'He was turning stiff and he was cold.'

'You're sure he was cold?'

'Yes: that's how I knew he was dead.'

'Then what did you do?'

'I called Sheriff Jefferson and he came out with Doc Mallard. Doc said Delaney had died around nine fifteen.'

'He judged that from the rigor and the temperature of the body?'

'I guess so.'

'Okay.' He got to his feet. 'I guess I've seen all I want here for the moment. Leave the set as it is, will you? I'll want to take another look at it.' He walked over to the window and stared at the view. 'It's a damn funny thing, but Maddox never seems to be wrong. There's something about this setup that doesn't jell. You can see that for yourself. That guy, Maddox! Come the time when I prove him wrong!'

I didn't say anything. My heart was beating sluggishly, and I felt scared.

'Well, I guess I'll have to poke around a little.' He held out his hand. 'I'll be seeing you. Where can I contact you?'

I gave him my telephone number and watched him write it down on the back of an envelope.

I said, 'You think there's something wrong with the claim?'

He grinned cheerfully at me.

'You think about it. You know as much as I do. The guy was paralysed. He couldn't have reached those screws. He couldn't have picked up that screwdriver. He was stone cold when you found him, and yet he had been dead only for three hours on a hot day, after getting a boosted electric shock through him. He had taken out an insurance policy a few days

81

before he died. By dying the way he did, his wife cashed in for five thousand bucks. Maybe it all happened the way it seems to have happened. I don't know.' He tapped me gently on my chest. 'We guys in the insurance racket are suspicious of anything that doesn't jell. I'm going to dig around and see if I can find anything else that doesn't jell. Then I'll know if this claim is a phoney or not. Maybe I'm wasting my time, but that's what I'm getting paid for. Be seeing you,' and nodding, he walked down to his smart, sleek Packard.

I watched him drive away, then slowly I walked back into the lounge.

This was a bad start, I told myself, but it didn't mean he could prove Delaney had been murdered. He would have to go a long way before he proved that. My plan hadn't been one hundred per cent foolproof, but at least, it hadn't entirely come apart.

I sat for some minutes, smoking and thinking.

I saw that much depended on Harmas not finding out that Gilda and I were lovers. If he found that out, he would have the motive: the wife, the crippled husband, the lover and five thousand dollars of insurance money. It was the perfect setup for murder.

I had to warn Gilda again to stick to the story I had given her: that she had gone down to Glyn Camp, that, on the way, she had had a flat, and she had been delayed while she had changed the tyre.

I decided I would go down to Los Angeles and call her from a pay booth.

I drove into Los Angeles soon after four o'clock. I went to a pay booth and rang her number, but there was no answer. I guessed she was out looking for a job. I hung around, killing time and I kept ringing the number. It wasn't until nearly seven that I got an answer.

I wasn't taking any chances. For all I knew they might have already tapped her line.

'Gilda: don't mention my name,' I said. 'Listen carefully. I'm calling from a pay booth. The number is 55781. I want you to go out to a pay booth and call this number. I'll be waiting. It's urgent.'

'But why can't we talk now?'

'Not on your line. Please hurry. Have you the number?'

'I have it.'

'I'll be waiting,' and I hung up.

I waited in the pay booth, smoking and sweating in the stuffy atmosphere for ten minutes. Then the bell rang and I lifted the receiver.

'Gilda?'

'Yes. What is all this, Terry? What is happening?'

'The insurance people are probing as I thought they would,' I said. 'They don't appear satisfied the way he died. We've got to be careful. I think they are watching you, Gilda. Now listen...'

'Terry! What are you talking about? Why should I care if they are watching me? I've done nothing to be ashamed of! You're keeping something from me! I've had that feeling ever since he died. I must know what it is!'

'It's just that we've got to be careful they don't find out about us, Gilda ... that's all.'

'I must see you, Terry!'

'No! I have an idea they are watching you. If they see us together, it will be the give away. We can't meet yet.'

'I'm going to see you, Terry! I'm going to see you tonight!'

'They may be watching you, Gilda,' I said. 'If they see us together...'

'Where are you now?'

'The drugstore on Figuroa and Florence.'

'Wait for me outside. I'll be along in the Buick in about an hour's time.'

'But listen, Gilda...'

'Oh, it'll be all right,' she said impatiently. 'I'll make sure no one is following me,' and she hung up.

It was a long wait.

A little before half-past seven, I left the drugstore and stood in the shadows. It was dark now. I wanted to go home, but I had an idea that if I didn't meet her ,now, she would come to my cabin and I knew that could be fatal.

Ten minutes later, the Buick Estate Wagon edged to the

kerb. I ran across, opened the door and slid in beside her. She forced the Buick back into the stream of traffic and drove on down the busy thoroughfare.

Neither of us said anything.

After a few moments, I looked back at the line of headlights behind us.

'No one is following us,' Gilda said. 'I made sure.'

'They're experts...'

'No one is following us!'

There was a curt snap to her voice I hadn't heard before, and I looked quickly at her.

In the lights of the passing street lamps, she looked pale and her expression set. She stared ahead, driving well, moving the big car through the gaps in the traffic, her foot touching the gas pedal every now and then to shoot us forward, ahead of the car in front of us.

We drove like that for twenty minutes or so, then we were clear of Los Angeles and we were heading into the open country, along the fast highway.

Still we said nothing.

Another twenty minutes driving brought us to a side road. She pulled off the highway onto the road, accelerated, driving fast, climbing the steep hill, and then, in a few minutes, she pulled onto one of those laybys, constructed specially for courting couples or for tourists who wish to see Los Angeles from the heights.

As she set the parking brake, I looked back down the long, twisting road, but there was no sign of any car coming up, only the gleam of many headlights far below as the traffic pounded out of Los Angeles.

Gilda turned in the driving seat and looked directly at me.

'Why are you so frightened, Terry?'

'I'm not frightened,' I said carefully. 'I'm anxious. This insurance claim was a mistake. The agent of the company has examined the set. He seems to think there is something suspicious about the claim.'

'Why should he think that?'

'Some business about it being difficult for your husband to

have taken the back off the set. It doesn't seem he could have reached the bottom fixing screws from his chair.'

'I told you: I am quite sure he didn't take the back off the set. It was something he would never do. It was you who said he did it.'

'Of course he took it off! When I got there, the back was off ...'

'I think the best thing I can do,' she said, not looking at me, 'is to tell Mr Macklin to withdraw the claim. I can manage without the money. I'll sell everything. There should be just enough to settle his bills.'

I stiffened.

'You mustn't withdraw the claim now!'

'Why not?'

'Once a claim is lodged, it has to go through, otherwise the insurance company will suspect fraud. They'll think you have withdrawn the claim because you have lost your nerve. If you withdraw the claim now, they are certain to tell the Los Angeles police.'

'Why should I care if they tell the police? I've got nothing to hide!'

'But you have! They could find out about us!'

'And what if they do?'

I drew in a long, slow breath. I thrust my fists between my knees, squeezing them hard.

'We've been over all that before, Gilda. We have got to be careful.'

'Is that why you asked me to call you from a pay booth?'

'Yes. I don't trust these insurance agents. They may have tapped your line.'

She swung around and stared at me, her eyes glittering.

'Tell me the truth!'

'What do you mean?'

'It wasn't an accident, was it? You've been trying to cover up something. You've got to tell me!'

I started to say it was an accident, then I stopped. All of a sudden, I felt I couldn't lie to her. I loved her. You can't lie to a woman who means as much as Gilda meant to me. I knew

85

it was a fatal thing to do, but I just couldn't keep it to myself any longer.

'No, Gilda: it wasn't an accident.' I began to shake. I killed him.'

She caught her breath in a quick gasp and moved away from me.

'You killed him?'

'I must have been out of my mind,' I said. 'I couldn't bear the thought of you being tied to him for the rest of his days. I couldn't bear the thought of you never being mine so long as he was alive – so I killed him.'

She sat motionless. I could hear her quick, uneven breathing.

'I did it because I love you, Gilda,' I said. 'With any luck, they won't find out. I'm hoping in a few months we can go away and start a new life together.'

She hunched her shoulders as if she were feeling cold.

'How did you do it?'

I told her.

I didn't hold anything back. I told her the whole sordid tale.

She sat in the corner of the car, her hands in her lap, motionless, staring out into the moonlit night, her big forget-me-not blue eyes wide and expressionless.

'If only that insurance claim hadn't been put in,' I said, 'I would have had nothing to worry about. But now ... I don't know. I think Harmas suspects something. That's why we mustn't see each other until the claim is settled.'

'What do you want me to do?'

Her voice was flat and cold.

'I want you to stick to the story you told Jefferson,' I said. 'That's all I want you to do. Harmas may question you. If he gets the slightest suspicion that we have been lovers, we shall be in trouble. We must keep away from each other until they have settled the claim.'

'You mean you will be in trouble, don't you? If I tell them the truth, there is no trouble for me.'

She was right, of course, but I just looked at her, not saying anything.

'All right: I'll lie for you. I'll stick to the story.' She sat for several seconds staring through the windshield. Then she said quietly, 'Would you mind walking back? You'll be able to get a lift on the highway. I would rather go back alone.'

My heart gave a little lurch.

'This is not going to make any difference to your feelings for me, Gilda? I love you. I need you now more than ever before.'

'This has been a shock. Will you leave me now please?'

I tried to take her hand, but she moved it quickly out of my reach.

I could see how white she was and how tense. I realized she had to be given time to get over what I had told her. Already I was bitterly regretting having told her.

I got out of the car.

'I wouldn't have done it, Gilda, only I love you so much'.

'Yes, I understand.'

The car began to move away from me. She was staring through the windshield. She didn't look at me.

I watched the red rear lights of the car go down the steep hill. I had a sudden horrible feeling she was moving away out of my life: moving out of it for good and all.

Chapter VII

I

Two days crawled by, and they were bad days for me.

I kept thinking of Gilda, seeing again the wooden stunned expression on her face as she had driven away and wondering why she hadn't wanted me with her.

I tried to assure myself it was a natural reaction. I had confessed that I had murdered her husband. The shock must have been a horrible one. What really bothered me now was that this stupid confession might have killed her love for me.

That was something I couldn't bear to think of, for her love was more precious to me than my own life.

On the second night I could stand my thoughts no longer. I got into the truck and drove down to Los Angeles. I called her number from a pay booth.

I was startled when a man answered.

'Is Mrs Delaney there?' I asked, wondering, with a feeling of dread, if this man was a police officer.

'Mrs Delaney left a couple of days ago,' the man said. 'I'm sorry but she didn't give us a forwarding address.'

I thanked him and hung up.

I didn't need a blueprint to tell me what **had happened. My** stupid confession had killed her love for me as I had feared it might. She had gone away because she didn't want to see me again – ever.

I scarcely slept that night, and for the first time, I regretted killing Delaney. I was paying for what I had done, and from the look of my future, I would go on paying for it.

The following morning, as I was shaving, the telephone bell rang.

It was Harmas calling.

'Can you meet me at Blue Jay cabin at eleven?' he asked.

'We're having a meeting, and I want you in on the technical end.'

I said I would be there.

'Swell, and thanks,' and he hung up.

The next three hours were bad ones. My nerves got so shaky I had a drink around half-past nine, and that led to three more drinks before I drove over to Blue Jay cabin.

Harmas's Packard was parked near the verandah steps, and as I walked up them, I could hear him whistling in the lounge.

He looked around as I paused in the doorway.

'Come on in. The others will be along any time now.' I walked stiff-legged into the lounge.

'What's it all about?' I asked.

'You're going to see how we insurance dicks earn our money,' Harmas said. He had dropped his indolent pose. He looked alert, and his wide, satisfied smile scared me. 'I want you to give me a hand.' He took two ten-dollar bills from his wallet and handed them to me. 'You'd better freeze onto these in advance in case I forget. My boss - this guy Maddox I was telling you about - is coming, and when he's around I'm likely to forget my own name.'

'Maddox?' That really jolted me. 'What's he coming for?'

'Here he is now,' Harmas said.

I heard a car coming and I stepped to the french doors and looked out.

The sight of the police car with its siren and red light on the roof gave me a shock.

From the car came Lieutenant John Boos of the LA Homicide Squad: a big, powerfully-built man, around forty-two or three, with a red, fleshy face and small steel-grey eyes.

He was followed by a short, thickset man who I guessed was Maddox. He wasn't more than five-foot six. He had the shoulders and chest of a prize fighter and the legs of a midget. His face was rubbery and red. His eyes were restless and as bleak as a Russian winter. He wore his well-cut clothes carelessly, and he had a habit of running thick, stubby fingers through his thinning grey hair to add to his untidy appearance.

He came up the verandah steps, frowning, his small restless eyes missed nothing.

Harmas introduced me.

Maddox shook my hand. His grip was hard and warm, and he nodded to me.

'Glad to have your help, Mr Regan,' he said. 'I understand you're working for the company now.'

I muttered something as Boos loomed up.

'Hello, Regan,' he said. 'So you've got tangled up in this thing too, huh?'   .

'That's right,' I said, and my voice sounded small and husky.

'Let's get at it,' Maddox said and walked into the lounge. He stood in front of the TV set. 'This it?'

'That's the baby,' Harmas said cheerfully. He turned the set around. 'Those four screws held the back in place.'

Maddox stared for a long moment, then walked over to the empty fireplace.

89

'Sit down, Lieutenant. You, Mr Regan, sit over there. We won't need you for a while so just take it easy.'

I sat away from the other three and I lit a cigarette. My heart was thumping and my hands were unsteady and I was pretty badly scared.

Boos picked the most comfortable chair and lowered his bulk into it. He took out a pipe and began to fill it.

Harmas sank into another lounging chair and stretched out his long legs.

'Well now, Lieutenant,' Maddox said, 'I've asked you up here because I'm not satisfied with this claim. Briefly, one of our salesmen called on Delaney and sold him insurance coverage for this TV set. There's a clause in the policy that gives coverage of five thousand dollars in the event of death through a fault in the set. It's one of those dumb clauses our sales people put in to catch a sale. We have sold twenty-three thousand, four hundred and ten of these policies, and this is the first claim covering death by a fault we have had. That is: it is a twenty-three thousand to one chance, and when that happens I get suspicious. The claim arrived five days after the policy was signed. Delaney was buried before the policy was even delivered.'

Boos lit his pipe and frowned at Maddox.

'It could be one of those things, Mr Maddox. I've read the coroner's report. I've talked to Sheriff Jefferson. Nothing I've seen in the report and nothing Jefferson has said has convinced me there's anything wrong with the setup. It looks straightforward enough to me.'

'It looks straightforward to you, Lieutenant, because you don't handle fifteen hundred claims a week as I do,' Maddox said. 'If you had sat at my desk for the number of years that I have, you would get to know a bad claim by instinct. I know this claim is a bad one. I feel it here!' And he paused to thump his chest. 'But I don't expect you to act on my hunches. Let's take a look at the setup. Delaney was paralysed from the waist down. I've got a report from the doctor who attended him when the accident happened. The doctor says he was not able to bend at the waist. That means he was sitting upright all the time in his chair, and he could not bend forward. Now I'll give you a little demonstration that'll interest you.'

He turned to me.

'Mr Regan, I want your help. Will you sit in Delaney's chair?'

I knew what was coming. Keeping my face expressionless, I walked over to the chair and sat in it.

Harmas picked up a length of cord that was lying on the table. He went around behind me and looped the cord around my chest and behind the chair and tied it tightly, preventing me from moving forward.

'That was the way Delaney was fixed: bolt upright and unable to bend forward,' Maddox said.

'Okay, okay,' Boos said, frowning. 'So what?'

'Go ahead, Regan,' Maddox said, 'and take the back off the set.

'It can't be done,' I said.

'Well, try anyway, and try hard.'

I wheeled the chair up to the set and took out the two top fixing screws: that was easy, but I couldn't get within two feet of the bottom screws, fixed as I was in the chair.

'You've read the coroner's report' Maddox said to Boos. 'When Regan found Delaney's body, the back of the set was off. And another thing there was a screwdriver by Delaney's side. He apparently got it from the storeroom. He hooked the toolbox down from the shelf with a walking stick. The tools fell on the floor. Ask yourself: how did he manage to pick the screwdriver up?'

Harmas put the screwdriver on the floor beside me.

'Can you reach it?'

My fingers were a good twelve inches from the tool.

Maddox said to Harmas, 'Take the back off the set.'

When Harmas had removed the back, Maddox said to Boos, 'See those two terminals in the set? Delaney was supposed to have touched them with the screwdriver: that's how he was supposed to have been killed. You can see Regan can't get near them from where he is sitting.'

Boos got abruptly to his feet. He came to stare at the inside of the set.

91

'Do you see what I'm driving at?' Maddox went on. 'Delaney is supposed to have taken the back off the set. He couldn't have done it. He is supposed to have got the screwdriver from the storeroom. He couldn't have done it. He is supposed to have touched those two terminals. He couldn't have done it.'

Boos stared at him.

'Well, I'll be damned!'

Harmas undid the cord that bound me to the chair and I got out of the chair.

Then Boos turned to me.

'Let's have your story again, Regan,' he said. 'Let's go over the whole thing. You called on Delaney to see how the set was working. Right?'

'Yes. I found Delaney lying in front of the TV set. There was a steel screwdriver by his hand and the back of the set was off. I thought he had electrocuted himself. I pulled the plug out of the mains and then I touched him.'

'He was dead?' Boos asked.

'Yes.'

'How did you know he was dead?'

'He was cold and he was stiff.'

'When a man is killed by a big dose of electricity,' Maddox said, 'he burns. He's not going to cool the way a body would cool, dying from gun-shot wounds or a stab in the back ' The jolt he gets from an electric shock would increase the temperature of his blood. If Delaney had died of an electric shock, his body wouldn't have been noticeably cold in three hours.'

Boos began to look bewildered.

'Are you trying to tell me he didn't die of an electric shock?' he demanded, staring at Maddox.

'I'm not trying to tell you anything,' Maddox said curtly. 'I want his body exhumed.'

Boos scratched the side of his neck, frowning at Maddox.

'You'll have to talk to Jefferson first,' he said. 'Maybe there is something wrong, but I'm Homicide. You're not suggesting Delaney was murdered, are you?'

There was a constriction in my chest now that made breathing difficult. I leaned forward in my chair, staring at Maddox, my hands squeezed between my knees, waiting to hear what he would say.

'Am I suggesting Delaney was murdered?' Maddox asked. 'No, I'm not suggesting it: I'm telling you he was murdered! He was murdered because he took out an insurance policy that covered his crippled life for five thousand dollars. He was murdered because his killer took into account that the inquiry would be handled by two old dead-beats who would accept what they saw and wouldn't dig deeper.' A hard, grim smile lit up his face. 'Murder? Of course it's murder! Why do you think I brought you out here? This is the plainest case of murder I've ever had to deal with!'

II

Boos scratched a match alight. The sound of the red head against the sanded side of the box made a sharp explosion in the silence of the room.

No one was looking at me. That was my good luck.

'Now look, Mr Maddox,' Boos said after he had lit his pipe and had got it to draw to his satisfaction, 'I know your hunches' I know you have yet to be proved wrong. Okay, if you say this is murder, I'll listen, but before I start something I can't finish, I want to be convinced.'

Maddox went back to the fireplace and stood before it.

'This is a murder case. When I smell murder, I know it's murder. I've never been wrong, and what's more, I'll stake my life I'm not wrong this time. Anyway, I can give you enough ammunition to blast this old has-been right out of office.'

Boos had let his pipe go out. As he groped for his matches, he said sharply, 'What ammunition?'

'I've given you enough to get an order to exhume the body, but I can give you more. I can even give you a guess who killed him.'

My heart missed a beat, then began to race so violently I could scarcely breathe.

'You can?' Boos was sitting forward, the match burning between his fingers, forgotten. 'Who killed him then?'

'His wife,' Maddox said. 'She's tried to kill him once before but only succeeded in crippling him.'

I started to protest but checked myself in time. I wanted to tell him he was crazy, but I hadn't the nerve. I knew if I spoke and they looked at me, they would know who had killed him all right. At that moment my guilt was written across my face.

'I don't get it,' Boos said.

'Delaney married this woman four years ago,' Maddox said. 'They hadn't been married three months before she got into touch with one of my agents. She suggested he should talk to Delaney about an accident insurance policy. She said her husband was interested in a hundred thousand coverage.' Maddox pointed a stubby finger at Boos. 'I don't have to tell you when a wife tries to arrange an accident policy for her husband the red light goes up. My agent told me. I told him to go ahead, but I opened a file on Mrs Delaney. The agent talked Delaney into signing a policy, but a day later, Delaney wrote in and cancelled it. We didn't press him because I smelt trouble. It was a hunch that paid off. Three days after he had cancelled the policy, my agent reported to me that Delaney had met with an accident. If he had been insured, I would have contested the claim and started an investigation, but as he wasn't insured I let Jarrett, who you took over from, handle it. It was cleverly done, and he didn't get anywhere. You'll find it on file though. Delaney was drunk and asleep and she was driving. She stopped the car on the mountain road. A friend of hers had had a breakdown and was blocking the road. Delaney was asleep. She got out of the car and her story was she hadn't set the parking brake properly. It's a wonder Delaney survived.'

Boos said, 'Well, I'll be damned!'

'The woman must be cock-eyed,' Maddox went on. 'The moment Delaney takes out this TV policy and she discovers he is covered for five thousand bucks, she moves in again: only this time she kills him, and this time I'm right here to fix her!'

This was the moment when I should have got to my feet

and told him he was wrong. This was the moment when I should have told him I had killed Delaney. But I didn't. I just sat there, my heart pounding, too frightened for my rotten skin to tell them the truth.

Boos tapped out his pipe.

'You can't prove she killed him, Mr Maddox.'

Maddox made an impatient gesture with his hands.

'That's your job. I'm telling you this is murder, and I'm willing to bet my last buck, she did it. It's your job to pin it on her. Find out where she was when Delaney died. I'll bet you she'll have an alibi. When you know what it is, take a good look at it before you accept it. Get Delaney's body exhumed. I'm willing to bet she staged the scene by taking off the back of the TV set and she also planted the screwdriver by Delaney, and she did it to collect the five thousand coverage.'

Boos stroked his fleshy nose.

'Well, okay, I'll talk to Jefferson. We'll have the body exhumed right away.' He got to his feet. 'Do you happen to know where Mrs Delaney is?'

Harmas said, 'She's in Los Angeles looking for work. Her attorney, Macklin, will know where you can contact her.'

'Okay, Mr Maddox,' Boos said. 'I'll take it from here. I'll let you know how it develops.' He turned to me. 'I'm going to lock up this place and seal it. I want the set left just where it is. Did she ask you to sell the set?'

'Yes.'

'Well, I'll talk to her.'

'Let me have a copy of the p.m. report,' Maddox said as he started for the door. He paused abruptly to look at me. 'You'll be needed as a witness for us, Mr Regan. Thanks for what you've done so far.'

He and Harmas went down to the Packard and drove away.

That left Boos and myself alone.

Boos stared after the departing Packard.

'That guy!' There was a note of admiration in his voice. 'What a police officer he would have made! He can smell murder a hundred miles away, and I've never known him to be wrong. Well, I'd better seal this joint up. You got the key?'

I handed him the key.

'Okay, Regan, be seeing you at the trial,' and he started down the passage to the back door, humming under his breath.

I left the cabin and got into my truck.

It wasn't until I was back in my cabin and had drunk two fingers of straight Scotch that I began to recover my nerve.

Could they prove a case against Gilda?

I knew Delaney had died by an electric shock. How could they hope to prove that Gilda had been responsible?

I would be crazy to give myself up until I knew for certain that she was in danger. I must wait and see what happened. Then, if it looked bad for her, I would tell Boos the truth.

The following afternoon I drove down to Glyn Camp. I left the truck in the parking lot and walked over to Jefferson's office.

I found him sitting at his desk, a bewildered, brooding expression in his eyes.

'Hello, son?' he said. 'Come on in and sit down.'

I sat down and watched him lift the jar of apple jack into sight from behind his desk. He poured two shots into glasses and pushed one of the glasses over to me.

'Well, the thing's happened I didn't want to happen,' he said. 'I had at the back of my mind that Delaney's death wasn't all that straightforward. If I had known he had signed that insurance policy, I would have made a much closer investigation.'

'What's going on?' I asked.

'They're holding the p.m. now. They've got Allison, the Medical Officer from LA, to handle it. They exhumed the poor fella last night.'

'You know Maddox thinks Mrs Delaney did it?' I said.

Jefferson nodded.

'There's a man I could never get along with. That girl wouldn't hurt a fly. I haven't been dealing with people for sixty years without learning who is a bad 'un and who isn't.

I'm willing to bet she didn't do it.'

'Me too.'

'I don't think it's murder,' Jefferson went on. 'I think it was suicide. She got tired of living with him and she left him. He was down to his last buck, and with her leaving him, it was too much for him. Somehow he managed to get the back off the TV set. Don't ask me how, but a desperate man can do things that most people think impossible.'

'Have they talked to her yet?' I asked.

'They can't find her. She's vanished.'

I stiffened, slopping my drink.

'Vanished? Doesn't Macklin know where she is?'

'No. He had a letter from her saying she was moving from the room she rented and was looking for somewhere else to stay. When she found something, she would let him know. That was three days ago. He hasn't heard from her, and Boos is hinting she's got in a panic and bolted.'

'Can't they trace her by her car?' 'She's sold it.'

The sound of heavy steps coming along the passage made both of us look sharply towards the door which jerked open.

Lieutenant Boos stood in the doorway. There was a smirking look of triumph in his close-set eyes. He came in, kicking the door shut.

'How do you like it?' he said, addressing Jefferson. 'The guy wasn't electrocuted at all!'

I sat forward, staring at him, scarcely believing I had heard aright.

Jefferson too was staring.

'If he wasn't electrocuted, then how did he die?' he asked, a croak in his voice.

'He was poisoned,' Boos said. He put two big, red hairy hands on Jefferson's desk, and leaning forward, went on, 'He was murdered! Someone fed him enough cyanide to wipe out half this goddam town!'

The big moon floated serenely in the night sky, casting a brilliant white light over my cabin and garden.

I sat on the verandah, smoking. The time was a little after ten o'clock.

I was still stunned by the news Boos had shot into our laps. I could scarcely believe that Delaney had died of poisoning and that I hadn't after all killed him. I was beginning now to savour the realization with an overwhelming feeling of relief that by a trick of fate I was not after all a murderer. The knowledge that I could now no longer be arrested, tried, found guilty and put in the gas chamber gave me a buoyant feeling of freedom.

But if it was good news for me, it was serious news for Gilda.

Not for one moment did I believe she had poisoned Delaney. I was sure Jefferson was right when he had said the thought of losing her and knowing he had no money left had been too much for Delaney. He had taken the easy way out - he had killed himself.

If I hadn't planned to kill him, if I hadn't gone to the cabin and set the stage so that it would look as if he had been electrocuted, Gilda would not be in the perilous position she was in now.

To save her, I might still have to tell the police what I had done. Attempted murder was a serious charge. I could get a twenty-year sentence. The thought turned me cold.

The sound of a car coming up the road brought me to my feet. I went to the verandah rail and watched Jefferson's old Ford bump up my drive-in.

He came slowly up the verandah steps.

'Come in and have a drink,' I said, wondering what he was doing up here.

He sat down while I made a couple of highballs. I looked at him. He was pulling at his moustache, a brooding expression in his eyes. I saw, with surprise, he wasn't wearing his sheriff's star. This was the first time since I had known him that he hadn't worn it.

He saw me staring and he smiled ruefully.

'I turned it in this afternoon. It's always better to walk out than to be kicked out.'

'You mean you have resigned office?'

'That's it. It's time I did. I've got beyond the job.' He took the highball. 'Truth to tell, now I've taken the plunge, it's a relief. I can sit on the fence and watch the other fella do the work. I'm sorry it finished this way. It's my own fault. I should have resigned years ago.'

'I'm sorry,' I said and I meant it.

'I didn't come up here to talk about myself. Have you heard about Mrs Delaney?'

A cold creepy sensation crawled over me.

'No, I haven't heard a thing.'

'They arrested her this afternoon in Los Angeles.'

I sat down abruptly.

'For God's sake!'

'She's being charged with the murder of her husband and attempted fraud. Maddox is pressing the charge: she's in a bad jam, Regan.'

I scarcely noticed that he called me by my surname and not my Christian name as he usually did.

'But she didn't kill him!'

'I don't think she did, but Boos has got quite a case against her. She admits buying the cyanide.'

That gave me a hell of a shock.

'She bought it?'

'Yes. She says she went to the pharmacist in Glyn Camp. There was a wasps' nest in the roof of the cabin, and she asked the pharmacist if he could give her something to kill the wasps. He gave her the cyanide. She signed the poison book. When she got home, she told Delaney she had bought the stuff. She put the poison in the desk drawer, meaning to fix the nest the next day, but she was busy and forgot about it. Boos has checked. The wasps' nest is there all right, but that doesn't alter the fact that she bought the poison. She's admitted quarrelling with Delaney the night before his death, and that he hit her. She admits making up her mind to leave him. She told Boos she had told Delaney that she intended to leave him. When she did leave him, he was very disturbed. On her way down to Glyn Camp, she had a flat. She took some time to fix it, then she went on to Glyn Camp. While she was fixing the flat, she had a change of mind about leaving her husband. By the time she got down to Glyn Camp, she had decided she couldn't leave a cripple to fend for himself, so she came back.

On the way back, she met you with the news he was dead. That's her story. I was there when she told it, and I believe it, but Boos doesn't.'

I drew in a long slow breath.

'Why doesn't he?'

'His theory is that when she found out Delaney hadn't any money left, she decided to kill him and grab the five thousand from the insurance. Maddox thinks so too. She denies knowing that Delaney was insured until after the funeral, when you gave her the letters you had been carrying around with you. Maddox says she is lying. He claims soon after her marriage with Delaney, she tried to persuade him to insure his life...'

'I know. I've heard that one,' I broke in. 'No jury would believe that once they looked at her.'

'Maybe you're right, but there's this TV setup. Both Maddox and Boos swear Delaney couldn't have taken the back off the set. I think he might have if he had been desperate enough, but that will be for the jury to decide. But the one damning thing even I can't explain away is if Delaney took poison, how did he get rid of the glass containing the poison?'

I stiffened to attention, staring at him.

'What do you mean?'

'The pharmacist sold the cyanide to Mrs Delaney in block form. To have used it as a poison it would have had to have been dissolved in water or whisky. Cyanide kills instantly. As soon as it got into his mouth, he'd die. There was no glass found beside him where you'd expect to find one. That must rule out suicide. It makes things pretty difficult for Mrs Delaney. Boos thinks she doped his whisky with the poison, then not thinking she removed the glass when he was dead. Boos says that is the kind of slip most killers could make.'

It was then, and only then, that I remembered the glass lying by Delaney's side when I had found him.

I had been afraid that the Coroner might have become suspicious if he had thought Delaney had been drinking and I had washed out the glass and put it away.

'There was a glass,' I said. 'I found it by his side. I washed it out and put it in the kitchen cupboard.'

Jefferson sat upright, staring at me.

'Is this true?'

'Yes, of course. I wouldn't lie about a thing like that. I can't think why I did it. Maybe subconsciously I didn't want it to come out at the inquest for Mrs Delaney's sake that her husband was a drunk. Anyway, that's what I did.'

Jefferson relaxed back in his chair. He began to pull at his moustache.

'I'm not a law officer any longer,' he said, 'so what I say doesn't matter, but I don't think Boos will accept that story. I don't think a jury would either.'

'But I tell you – it's true!' I said, my voice shooting up. 'I'm willing to go into court and swear to it!'

He stared up at the moon for some moments, frowning, then he said, 'As I said just now, Regan, I'm no longer a law officer. So what I say doesn't matter. But if I was still Sheriff I'd begin to wonder about you. I'd begin to wonder about you and Mrs Delaney.'

'What the hell do you mean?' I said, turning hot and then cold.

'Never mind. This is what you do: go down to Los Angeles first thing in the morning and talk to her attorney, Macklin. He's a smart fellow. He'll know how to handle it. Will *you* do that?'

'Yes. But, look, I don't understand...'

'Better not say anything to Boos about finding the glass,'

Jefferson went on, not looking at me. 'If he asks you, you'll have to tell him, but don't volunteer any information. You talk to Macklin first.' He suddenly stared hard at me. 'Whatever you say to him will be treated in confidence.'

I couldn't meet his searching, steady stare.

'I'll see him tomorrow.'

He got to his feet.

'I don't think she killed him,' he said. 'She's a nice girl. She wouldn't have poisoned him. All the same there's something badly wrong with the setup. If Delaney didn't take the back off the set, someone did, and that someone would be a man. No woman would think up a stunt like that. I'm glad I'm sitting on

101

the fence, Regan. I'm glad I don't have to handle this investigation.'

He nodded, then walked down the steps and got into his Ford.

It wasn't until he had driven away that I realized he hadn't shaken hands with me.

This was the first time since I had known him that he had failed to do that.

Chapter VIII

I

THE next morning I went down to Los Angeles and saw George Macklin.

He listened in silence to my story about finding the glass by Delaney's side.

When I was through, I said, 'This should put her in the clear, Mr Macklin, shouldn't it?'

'I wouldn't go as far as that,' Macklin said. 'It will help. It was a great pity you didn't remember it sooner. It would have carried a lot more weight if you had told Boos as soon as he knew Delaney had been poisoned. I want you to go over to police headquarters right away and tell him what you've told me. It's important you get it in first before you are asked.'

'I'll go now,' I said and started to get to my feet.

'Just a moment, Mr Regan.' His alert, shrewd eyes looked fixedly at me. 'I must warn you that evidence of this kind has value only if it is given by a disinterested witness. Are you disinterested?'

I found my eyes shifting away from his.

'If you mean do I want Mrs Delaney to go free, then of course I'm interested,' I said.

'I don't mean that at all.' His voice was sharp. 'When you tell Boos about finding the glass, you'll put yourself under a spotlight. This is evidence that could upset the case they have against Mrs Delaney. It's belated evidence and you have no proof to support your evidence. Boos will immediately wonder if you are lying to get her off. He'll wonder if there has been an association between Mrs Delaney and yourself. It would suit him very well if he could discover there was such an association. He'll check. Is there any chance at all that he may find evidence that you are an interested party?'

I thought bleakly of the Italian restaurant. What a fool I had been to have taken her there!

'I have been friendly with Mrs Delaney,' I said. 'Her husband knew it, of course. I took her to a restaurant one evening, but that was the only occasion we have been out together.' 'Did you meet anyone you knew?'

'No. It was an out-of-the-way place. I'm sure no one saw us who knew us.'

He thought for a long moment, then shrugged his shoulders.

'We'll have to take the risk. If he asks you if you have been friendly with Mrs Delaney, you had better tell him that you once met her out and you had dinner with her. It would be quite fatal for her if he found out you two had been to this restaurant and you had already told him you hadn't ever taken her out. You see, Mr Regan, Mrs Delaney's position is very uncertain. I am relying on the fact that there's not the slightest suspicion of scandal in her life. I intend to present her to the jury as a loyal, faithful wife who, in spite of the treatment she received from her husband, stuck to him for four years, and even when she was assaulted and had left him, she hadn't the heart to make a final break, and she returned to him. That is a picture that will make an impression on the jury. On the other hand, if the District Attorney can prove that she was unfaithful to Delaney during his lifetime, then I very much doubt if anything can save her.'

'Do you think you'll get her off?' I asked anxiously.

'I don't know. If she had some money, I would get Lowson Hunt to defend her. I think this case needs a man like Hunt.'

'What would it cost?'

Macklin shrugged his shoulders.

103

'I'd say around five thousand.'

'You think he could get her off?'

'If he can't, then no one can.'

I didn't hesitate.

'Okay: go ahead and hire him.'

Macklin laid down the letter opener and stared at me.

'What do you mean?'

'I said go ahead and hire him. I'll foot the bill.'

'Am I to understand you are offering to pay for Mrs Delaney's defence?' The words had a cold, clipped ring.

'That's right,' I said. 'I can go up to five thousand, but no more.'

I would have to sell pretty well everything to meet the bill, but I didn't care. I had got Gilda into this mess, and I was determined to get her out of it.

'You realize of course that it would be fatal to Mrs Delaney's interests if it was known you were financing her defence?'

'I'm not so stupid as to talk about it. You get Hunt; and I'll pay.'

'I'll see him. How can I get into touch with you?'

I gave him my telephone number.

After he had written it down, he said, 'Now if you'll go over to police headquarters...'

'Sure.'

I was aware he was looking oddly at me, but I didn't care. I left him and drove over to police headquarters.

I was feeling pretty nervous when I asked for Lieutenant Boos, and I was still more nervous when I was taken to his office.

Boos was smoking his pipe and standing by the window, staring down at the traffic. He turned when I came in.

'Hello, Regan. What can I do for you?'

'It's about Delaney's death,' I said. 'There's something I forgot to tell you. When I found him, there was an emty glass lying by his side. I washed it out and put it in the kitchen cupboard.'

Boos stood stock-still, staring at me; his small eyes flinty.

'What the hell did you do that for?'

'I don't know. I was badly shocked. I did it while I was waiting for Jefferson. I kicked against the glass and picked it up. It gave me something to do: took my mind off finding Delaney. I'd forgotten about it, then this morning I remembered.'

Boos' face went a deep purple.

'Are you kidding me?' he snarled.

'No. I'm telling you: there was an empty drinking glass lying by his side. I wouldn't kid about a thing like that.'

'You mean to tell me you've just remembered it?'

'That's right.'

He blew out his checks.

'Pretty damned convenient for Mrs Delaney, isn't it?'

'Is it? I remembered it, and I came down here right away to tell you.'

'Yeah?' He moved around his desk. Listen, Regan, if you're lying, you could go down on an accessory rap! And I'm telling you, I think you are lying!'

I kept control of myself with an effort.

'Why should I lie?' I said. 'I found the glass by his side!

If you don't believe me, then it's your look out!'

He stood for a moment glaring at me, then he said, 'Okay.' He went to the door, opened it and bawled for Hopkins, his sergeant. 'We'll go out there right away, and you'll show me where you found the glass and where you put it.'

Hopkins, a thin, tall man with a stoop, came in.

'We're going out to Delaney's place,' Boos said to him.

'This joker here has suddenly remembered finding an empty drinking glass beside Delaney's body which he picked up, washed out and put away. Can you imagine?'

'Is that a fact?' Hopkins said, gaping at me.

'Let's go and find out,' Boos said grimly.

We drove in silence all the way up to Glyn Camp and to Delaney's place. I sat at the back of the police car: Boos and Hopkins in the front.

It was a nervy, uncomfortable drive for me. I could feel the hostility of the two men in their rigid silence.

When we got to the cabin, I showed them where I had

found the glass, then I showed them the glass in the kitchen cupboard.

Boos wouldn't let me touch it. He carefully put a handkerchief around it, lifted it and sniffed at it.

'I washed it out,' I said.

'Yeah: I heard you the first time.'

He gave the glass to Hopkins who put it in a cellophane bag and then into his pocket.

'Okay, Regan,' Boos said, suddenly the very tough cop, 'what's this woman to you?'

I was expecting this and I was ready braced for it.

'She was nothing to me,' I said before I could stop myself or think of Macklin's warning. 'She was just the wife of a client.'

'Yeah?' Boos sneered. 'With a body like that? Listen: you came up here to sell a TV set and you fell for her, didn't you? I would have done the same. That woman's got everything, and you knew she wasn't getting any loving. So you picked on her. That's it, isn't it?'

I wanted to plant my fist in his sneering face, but I controlled myself. I knew he was needling me to make me blurt out a damaging admission.

'You're wrong. She was nothing to me.'

'I say yes.' His small eyes glittered. 'Will you swear you never took her out? Never lusted after her? Never had her alone to yourself?'

Then I remembered Macklin's warning. He had said it would be fatal to Gilda if I lied about taking her to the Italian restaurant and Boos found out. But I couldn't tell him now. I knew, if I did, he would get the truth out of me. I knew too he would jump it on Gilda and she might deny it.

I had to take the risk of him finding out.

'I swear to that,' I said. 'She was nothing to me!'

He stared at me for a long moment, then turned away.

'For your sake, Regan, I hope you're not lying. I'm going to check. If I find out you are lying, you're going down for an accessory rap, and if I don't get you fifteen years, I'll turn my badge in.'

I felt I was over the danger now – anyway for the time being.

'To hell with you, Lieutenant,' I said. 'You can do what you damn well like.'

He suddenly grinned.

'Okay, Regan. Maybe she wasn't such a dope as to remove the glass. I always thought it was crummy the glass wasn't there. Well, we'll see. Come on: I'll drive you back.'

II

Two days later I had a telephone call from Macklin.

'Hunt is taking the case,' he said. 'He wants to talk to you. Will you be at his office at eleven this morning?'

I said I would.

Macklin sounded curt and unfriendly, and after he had given me Hunt's address, he hung up.

Lowson Hunt had a set of offices in the fashionable quarter of Los Angeles. I knew him by reputation as did anyone who read the murder cases in the papers over the past ten years.

I had never seen him, and I was surprised to find that he was small, thin and frail looking. He could have been anything from fifty to sixty years of age. His thin pale face was nondescript: it was only his eyes that gave a hint of the man behind the mask. They were remarkable eyes: small and washed out and blue, but they gave me the impression of being able to look through a wall and see well beyond it: the most disconcerting eyes I have ever had to meet.

'Sit down, Mr Regan,' he said, waving to a chair. He made no attempt to get up or to shake hands. 'I've been through the case against Mrs Delaney. I understand you are offering to finance her defence.'

'That's right.'

I then got the full blast from his eyes, and the searching stare made me move uneasily.

'Why?'

'That's my business,' I said curtly. 'What's it going to cost?'

He leaned back in his chair, resting his small white hands on the desk, and continued to stare at me.

'It happens to be my business if you want me to get Mrs 'Delaney off,' he said. 'Let me explain: when I started to try to make a reputation for myself as a defending attorney, I had the bad luck to run up against Maddox of the National Fidelity. I was defending a man who was charged with the murder of his wife. She was insured, and the money came to him. There wasn't much of a case against him, and I felt confident that I'd get an acquittal, but I was wrong. When Maddox got on the stand and began sounding off about his instincts for spotting a phoney claim I could see the jury sliding away from me. Simply by stating facts and figures over the period he had been investigating claims, Maddox put so much suspicion into the minds of the jury that my client went to the gas chamber. During my career I have come up against Maddox three times, and each time he has licked me. I've accepted the fact now that he is an expert witness; he can sway juries and he is a deadly danger to anyone standing trial for murder. Maddox has been able to lick me because in every case he has been right. He has this odd instinct that tells him long before he even digs up the evidence that a claim is a phoney, and that the man or woman insured by his company has been murdered. He has sent eleven men and five women to the gas chamber during the past ten years. He now has a reputation that is almost impossible to shake. The jury and the press know that when he is connected with a prosecution the man or the woman on trial is a goner.' He drummed on the desk while he continued to stare at me. 'He has never been proved wrong for the simple reason he isn't ever wrong. Maddox says Delaney was murdered, and that means Delaney was murdered. It's my job when defending a client to get him off whether he is guilty or not. I don't give a damn how guilty he is. When he hires me, I'm his. body and soul, until he either walks out of a court a free man or goes to the gas chamber. I'm telling you this because, if I am going to lick Maddox, I must have the whole truth and all the facts. Whatever you tell me won't go beyond this room. It's up to you. It's your money. If you want to save her, you'll have to give me the facts.' He pointed a finger at me. 'But remember this: even if I get all the facts, I'm still not guaranteeing that I'll save her. I have had three failures against Maddox. I'm determined to lick him before I quit this racket, and this case may be my chance. I don't give a damn if Mrs Delaney did murder her husband. All I care about is pricking Maddox's ego. Once I show that he can be wrong, I've got him where I want him. No jury will be impressed with him as they have been in the past. It's going to make my other cases in which Maddox is involved a lot easier for me.' He paused, then went on, 'So if you have anything to tell me that I should know, now's the time.'

I hesitated for about three seconds, then I told him. I gave him the whole story from the moment I first met Gilda to the last time I saw her. I held nothing back, and it was a relief to get the whole thing off my mind.

He sat listening, not moving, his eyes fixed on the paperweight on his desk.

When I was through, he got abruptly to his feet and began to prowl around his big office, his hands in his trousers pockets, his face looking leaner than ever.

'That guy's instinct for smelling murder!' he said. 'It's fantastic!'

'But she didn't kill him,' I said. 'He killed himself.'

He turned to look at me.

'That was your luck. The setup was for murder, and Maddox spotted it. I'm not so sure that what you've told me couldn't make it tougher for her. The DA is going to prove that Delaney was a drunk. He's got the maid who worked there who'll tell the court Delaney began to hit the bottle as soon as he got up in the morning and went on hitting it. He's going to show that Mrs Delaney could have put the cyanide in his whisky which killed him instantly. Now that you've claimed to have found the glass, the DA is going to say she washed the glass out, then rinsed it in whisky and put it by his side. You spoilt that planted clue of hers by absentmindedly picking up the glass and putting it away. He is going to show that it was Mrs Delaney who arranged the TV set so that it looked as if he had electrocuted himself. If it gets out that you two were lovers, there's not a thing I can do for her. I've got to make the jury believe she was loyal and faithful to him and because he had no more money, he took his life.'

'That's how it did happen!' I said. 'They've got to believe it!'

'Well, we'll see. You can leave it to me now. Everything depends on whether the police find out you two were lovers. If they do, both of you are sunk. If they don't, then she has a chance. Now remember this, if she is found guilty, they won't send her to the gas chamber. She'll get maybe ten years. So don't do anything crazy like confessing, because it won't help her. She'll get a longer sentence, and you'll be in trouble too.'

'Well, okay,' I said uneasily. 'How about paying you? Do you want money now?'

'No. When it's over and the excitement's died down, I'll want five thousand bucks from you. But right now I'm going to put out the story that I am so sure Maddox has made a mistake this time that I'm going to defend her for nothing just for the satisfaction of proving Maddox is wrong. The press know all about the fights I've had with Maddox. They'll lap up a story like that. It'll also make an impact on the jury. You leave all that to me. I'll go and talk to her this afternoon.'

I went back to my cabin.

Soon after the trial, I would have to find five thousand dollars to pay Hunt. To raise the money I would have to part with practically every dime I had saved. I would be cleaned out.

I would have to leave Glyn Camp after the trial and it wouldn't be possible now for me to start again on my own. I would have to find a job, and there and then I wrote to a firm in Miami I had had dealings with, asking them if they could make use of my services.

There was nothing for me to do now but to wait the outcome of the trial and to hope Boos wouldn't find out about the Italian restaurant.

I wanted badly to write to Gilda, but I didn't dare.

She was in my mind, night and day, day and night, and I wondered continually if she was thinking of me.

Not knowing now how she felt about me tormented me.

110

III

Five weeks after Gilda's arrest, on a hot September morning, the trial opened in an atmosphere of tension and excitement.

Those five weeks had been anxious ones for me, but as the days passed and I heard nothing from the police, I began to feel more confident that they hadn't found out about us nor had anyone apparently recognized Gilda at the Italian restaurant - and they would have done I felt sure, for, by now, every newspaper carried photographs of her.

As one of the principal witnesses for the prosecution I was kept in the witness room away from the court during the opening proceedings.

The other witnesses waiting with me were Delaney's Mexican maid, Maria, Sheriff Jefferson, Doc Mallard, the pharmacist who had sold Gilda the cyanide and a fat, important looking man I hadn't seen before who kept to himself.

There was a police officer in the room and he didn't allow us to talk. I could see poor old Doc looked pretty shaky and unhappy and he had lost all his arrogance.

Jefferson was grim-faced, and he just nodded to me and then studiously avoided looking at me. I didn't blame him. I knew he had guessed I had had something to do with Delaney's death, and it was through me to a large extent that he had been forced to resign.

It wasn't until half-past two in the afternoon that I got my call, and that was after Doc Mallard, Jefferson and the pharmacist had been called.

I braced myself.

I hadn't seen Gilda now for six weeks and I remembered Hunt's warning.

As I walked down the corridor towards the courtroom I asked the police officer escorting me how the trial was going.

'That guy Maddox!' he said. 'This is the fourth time he's tangled with Lowson Hunt and from the look of it, he's scored again. You should have heard him sound off. By the time he was through with his figures and his hunches, the jury was looking away from her, and that's always a bad sign.'

111

As I walked into the courtroom, I didn't look at Gilda. It wasn't until I had taken the oath that I glanced in her direction.

My heart gave a lurch when I saw how strained and pale she was. But she looked beautiful. I had never seen her look more beautiful, and I longed to go to her and take her in my arms.

She didn't look at me and that hurt. She sat motionless beside Hunt, staring down at her hands.

I glanced over at the jury. They were a dead-looking lot: three of them women, the rest men. They stared at me, their eyes bored.

The DA got up and began questioning me about the TV set.

I went through the story of how I had found Delaney and why I had assumed he had died from an electric shock.

The DA took me over the story about finding the glass.

The jury now lost their bored expressions and I could see they were listening intently.

'I believe there was an experiment carried out by you and Mr Harmas,' the DA said, 'to do with the removing of the back of the set. Would you tell the jury just what this experiment was, Mr Regan?'

'Mr Harmas seemed to be under the impression that Delaney, paralysed as be was, couldn't have reached the bottom fixing screws that held the back of the set in place,' I said. 'I tried to remove the screws from Delaney's wheel chair and had great difficulty in reaching the screws.'

'Is it not a fact,' the DA said, 'that when you were tied into the chair you couldn't get anywhere near these screws? Nor could you pick up the screwdriver that was lying on the floor?'

'That's right,' I said, and I had to make an effort not to look at Gilda.

The DA wasn't satisfied with that. He took me over the experiment again in different words, asking questions, enlarging, and generally hammering into the minds of the jury that Delaney could not have taken off the back of the set nor could he have picked up the screwdriver.

At last he seemed satisfied he had made his point and he stepped back.

'Okay, Mr Regan, that's all,' he said, and glanced at Hunt.

Without even bothering to get out of his chair, Hunt said he had no questions to ask me, but he would call me later.

I was taken out to spend another hour in the stuffy little witness room; this time on my own.

I heard from my police escort that the DA called Harmas after I had gone and took him through the story of the experiment.

It was on this business of taking the back off the set that the case against Gilda rested, and the DA hammered it home.

Around four o'clock I was called into the courtroom. There was an atmosphere in the room you could lean against.

The fat, important looking man who had been in the witness room was on the stand. He told Hunt that his name was Henry Studdley, and he was a specialist in the diseases of the spine. He said Delaney had been his patient.

He explained that there was nothing unusual about Delaney's disability. His spine had been injured resulting in total paralysis from the waist down. Hundreds of people had been disabled in car accidents as Delaney had been disabled.

'Much has been made by the District Attorney.' Hunt said, 'of the fact that Delaney could not have reached the two lower screws on the set. It is on this point that my client is being, tried. I want to get this clear, doctor. Tell me, in your opinion, would it have been possible for Delaney, seated in his chair, to have removed those two bottom screws?'

'It would have been quite impossible for him to have reached the screws,' Studdley said emphatically.

This caused a major sensation, and the DA, thinking that Hunt had walked into a trap of his own making, was scarcely able to suppress a guffaw.

Hunt seemed quite unperturbed. He thanked Studdley, and asked him to step down, but not to leave the courtroom. Then he turned to the jury.

He said he was satisfied that Delaney had committed suicide.

Delaney was a drunkard and unstable. He and his wife had quarrelled the night before he died. He had assaulted her.

113

Although she had put up with his evil temper and his drinking habits for the past four years, loyally doing her duty as his wife, this was the final straw. She decided to leave him, Delaney knew his money was exhausted. When he was on his own, realizing he now had no wife nor money, he decided to kill himself. He knew that if he arranged things to look as if he had died accidentally his wife would come in for the insurance money, and she would be able to clear his debts. That was what he had done.

I could see the jury wasn't impressed by this theory. The DA's constant reminder that Delaney couldn't have taken off the back of the TV set made Hunt's suggestion a waste of time.

'I am in the position to demonstrate to you how Delaney got hold of the screwdriver and how he did in fact take off the back of the set,' Hunt went on. 'I would like to put Dr Studdley on the stand again.'

While Studdley walked to the stand, I saw the jury were showing interest and the DA was scowling at Hunt.

'Three days ago, doctor,' Hunt said to Studdley, 'I telephoned you and asked you to arrange something for me. Would you tell the court what it was I asked you to do?'

'You asked me to find a patient who had the exact symptoms that Delaney had,' Studdley said.

'And did you find such a patient?'

'Certainly. It wasn't difficult. I have at least six patients under my care who have exactly the same symptoms as Delaney had.'

Hunt turned to the judge and asked permission for the patient to take part in a demonstration.

The DA got to his feet, roaring objections.

There was a legal huddle between the judge, Hunt and the DA. Finally, it was decided that the DA should have the opportunity of examining the case papers of Delaney and the patient from Studdley's clinic and to call his own medical expert to watch the demonstration which was to be held at Blue Jay cabin.

On that note the court adjourned for the day.

IV

The following morning there was a big gathering in the lounge of Blue Jay cabin. Besides the judge and jury, there were the two medical experts, Boos, Maddox, Hunt, the DA and myself.

Seated in Delaney's wheel chair was a thin, delicate looking man whose name was Holman.

Hunt asked him to go to the storeroom and see if he could get a screwdriver from the toolbox.

Holman trundled himself down the passage, followed by the jury and anyone else who could squeeze into the crowded passage.

As a witness for the prosecution, I got a front row view.

We all watched Holman manoeuvre the chair into the storeroom and hook the stick over the side of the toolbox. He took a little time judging the distance and moved the chair slightly closer to the shelf. Then he tipped the box over.

The box fell slap in his lap. Several of the tools spilled out onto the floor, but both screwdrivers remained in his lap.

'You see,' Hunt said mildly. 'It was really very simple. The screwdriver never reached the floor.'

He got Holman to do the trick five times, and each time the screwdrivers dropped into Holman's lap,

I could see the DA was looking uneasy by now and the jury were glancing at each other significantly.

'Now we'll see about taking the back off the set,' Hunt said. 'Let's return to the lounge.'

We all followed Holman as he trundled the chair along the passage.

Hunt said to him, 'See if you can reach those two screws, Mr Holman.'

Holman wheeled the chair up to the set.

'It can't be done,' he said as he put out his arm. He was at least eighteen inches from the screws.

'Okay,' Hunt said quietly. 'Now I want you to imagine you are a desperate man and no matter how much it hurts, no matter how great the effort, it is essential for you to get at those two screws. I want you to imagine that, after you have taken the screws out, then you are going to commit suicide.'

A glass of water was put on an occasional table by Holman's side.

'Now go ahead,' Hunt said. 'Try to get at those screws.'

There was a sudden tension in the room that you could feel. Sweat trickled down my face as I leaned forward, my eyes, like everyone's eyes, glued on the man in Delaney's chair.

Holman manoeuvred his chair close to the TV set. Then he put his hands on the arms of the chair and raised his helpless body a few inches off the seat of the chair. He remained like that for several seconds. He then dipped his head forward and at the same time gave the chair a little push back. The chair slid away from him as he let go of the arms.

Before anyone could move, he had pitched forward, coming to the floor with a sickening crash.

A police officer started forward, but Hunt stopped him.

The fall had obviously badly shaken Holman, who lay motionless face down before the TV set.

Hunt went to him and squatted down beside him.

'Are you all right, Mr Holman?' he asked, an anxious note in his voice.

'Yes, I'm all right.'

The thin, shaky voice was a whisper in the room.

Then the paralysed man began to move slightly. He pushed himself over on his side. By him was the screwdriver. He picked it up, then undid the two fixing screws and pulled off the back of the set. From where he **lay he had no trouble in** reaching the two screws.

While everyone in the room watched him in tense and utter silence, he rolled onto his other side, reached out and picked up the glass of water. He drank a little of the water, then dropped the glass as he sank face down on the floor.

'Hold it!' Hunt said. He looked around the lounge until he spotted me. 'Mr Regan! Come here, please.'

I joined him beside Holman's motionless body.

'Look at this man. Was that how you found Delaney? Look at him carefully. Was that how you found him?'

'Yes,' I said. 'That was just the way he was lying.'

And that was the turning point of the trial.

Back in the courtroom that afternoon, the DA put up a fight, but he knew he was licked. Hunt had created too much doubt in the minds of the jury. His closing speech was powerful and stirring. He said that no man nor woman with any sense of responsibility could convict Gilda on such flimsy evidence and he demanded an immediate acquittal.

The jury were out for two hours.

They were the longest two hours I have ever lived through. When they came back, they all looked at Gilda, and I knew that she was free.

The foreman said they found her not guilty, and there was quite a demonstration in court.

Gilda stood beside Hunt. She was very white, and I could see she was breathing quickly by the rise and fall of her breasts.

When she left the courtroom, she didn't look in my direction and I hurried after her, but I lost her in the crowd.

As I was pushing my way to the exit, I bumped into Maddox, who grinned at me, his expression wolfish.

'That was a neat trick,' he said. 'She was lucky. Well, she didn't get my money, and that's what I care most about.'

Lowson Hunt joined him.

'This time you were wrong,' he said, his thin face showing his triumph. 'I knew I'd get her off.'

'Wrong?' Maddox said. 'She was saved by a trick. I'll say, I wasn't wrong! She's as guilty as hell!'

Leaving Hunt staring after him, Maddox walked down the steps to where his car was waiting.

Chapter IX

I

I HAD had a letter from the radio engineering firm in Miami who said that they could fit me into their organization.

Although the money they offered was lower than I had been earning on my own, I had decided to take the job as it would get me out of California, and it would give me a living until I could look around for something better.

It was my great hope and my wish that Gilda would come with me. I had no idea where she was staying in Los Angeles. As soon as I got back to my cabin, I called George Macklin and asked him where I could find her.

He was abruptly hostile.

'I can't give you Mrs Delaney's address. She left a few hours ago for New York. If you care to write to her, I will have the letter forwarded to her.'

This news that Gilda had gone to New York was a real jolt to me until I realized that she probably was trying to escape all the publicity and the newspaper men, and when she knew of my plans, she would join me.

I said I would write.

When I sat down to write the letter, I found the task harder than I had imagined. There was so much I wanted to say to her and so much I wanted to explain.

I told her I was going to Miami and I gave her my address there. I explained about the job. I said I loved her; that I wanted her to join me and I wanted us to start a new life together. I said I hoped she would feel she could love me again now that she knew I hadn't been responsible for Delaney's death. I asked her to write me in Miami, saying she was going to join me.

On my way down to the station to take the train to Miami, I left the letter at Macklin's office.

I settled down quickly in Miami. I had a two-room apartment, and I worked hard, but there was no joy in life for me, for I didn't hear from Gilda. I wrote again to her and sent the letter to Macklin. He didn't bother to acknowledge it.

Every time the postman came, I rushed to the door, hoping that a letter would be there from her. Every time the telephone bell rang I had the same sensation, hoping that she was calling from New York to say she had decided to join me.

But she didn't write and she didn't call, and after three months, I realized I had lost her. That was the time I really suffered for what I had done. I loved her, and to lose a woman one loves is something a lot worse than pain.

After a year, the ache had gone, but I still thought of her. By this time I was in charge of the department dealing with custom-made radio sets and I was making a reasonable living.

Fifteen months after the trial, fifteen months of not hearing a word from her, I was called to the boss's office, and he asked me how I would like to open a branch shop in New York, selling discs and custom-made sets.

It was a chance I wasn't likely to refuse. At the end of the month, I packed my things, left a forwarding address with the woman who had an apartment next to mine and flew up to New York.

Here at last, I told myself, I was within reach of Gilda. Even after those long, dreary fifteen months, I was still in love with her and continually thought of her. If I were lucky enough to meet her, I still hoped to be able to persuade her to marry me.

It was an odd sensation to find myself living in the same city as she and never knowing if I would run into her. It brought back the ache in my heart.

Then one day, fate or whatever you like to call it, took a hand.

A customer of mine who came to the shop pretty often to buy Long Play records decided one afternoon he would like to buy a custom-made radiogram.

His name was Henry Fuller. He was short and fat, and nearly seventy as made no difference. He was rich. I could tell that by his clothes, his manner and the chauffeur-driven Cadillac, so when he began to talk about a custom-made set, I knew I was heading for a big order.

I told him what I could build for him, and I didn't cut my corners. I said the best thing, if he were interested, was for me to come out to his place and look at the room and find out what the acoustics were like.

'You do that, Regan,' he said, and I could see he was pleased. He was the kind of man who expected service and didn't care what he paid for it. 'You run out this afternoon. I won't be there; but my wife will. I'll tell her you are coming.'

Because it was the rule of the firm to make sure of the customer's rating before building expensive sets, I called the Credit Investigation people and asked for a report on Fuller.

They told me he was a first-class risk. He was a stockbroker and worth at least four million dollars. He had a swank apartment on Riverside Drive. He had been married three times, and he had married his third wife only six months ago.

Fuller's apartment was a penthouse job with a magnificent roof garden and a splendid view over the City.

The wrought-iron front door was opened by an English butler who looked as if he had stepped out of the movies.

He took me into a lounge that was every inch of forty feet long. The decor was typically eighteenth century in style, extremely elegant, and the walls were panelled with carved pine. A quiet, luxurious richness brooded over the room that was set off by two big Italian Renaissance paintings that looked good enough to be genuine.

The butler left me in the lounge and crossed the hall into another room.

I heard him say, 'The person, madam, is here about the radio.'

A woman said, 'All right Harkness, I'll see him,' and the butler went away.

The sound of the woman's voice sent a creepy sensation through me.

Then Gilda came into the room.

She stopped abruptly and stared at me.

She was wearing a bottle-green dress with leather tags at the collar and pockets: a simple thing, but its cut shouted its price.

120

Her bronze-coloured hair was now piled high on the top of her beautifully shaped head. Her make-up was flawless. Around one of her wrists was a heavy gold bangle set with semi-precious stones. She looked wonderful.

For perhaps a second, bewilderment, fear and then anger chased across her face. Then she recovered herself, and her face became expressionless and wooden.

'What are you doing here?' she asked as she moved into the room, carefully shutting the door behind her.

'Gilda! I've been looking every place for you! Didn't you get my letters?'

The sight of her set my heart thumping and I started towards her.

'Keep away from me!'

The tone in her voice brought me to a standstill as if I had run into a brick wall.

'Why didn't you write, Gilda? I've been waiting and hoping...' I stopped as I saw her eyes travelling over me critically and contemptuously.

I knew I didn't strike much of a figure. My suit and shoes were shabby, and my hands were none too clean. I was a radio engineer: no more, no less, and I was out of place against this background of richness and luxury.

'What are you doing here?' she demanded.

'I've come about the radiogram. Gilda! Don't look at me like that! For God's sake - I love you!' Then I paused, frowning at her. 'But what are you doing here? Are you his secretary?'

'No. I am his wife.'

I felt as if someone had stepped up to me and had slugged me under the heart.

'You mean you're Fuller's wife?' I said. 'You married that old ruin? You? I don't believe it!'

'I am Mrs Henry Fuller,' she said, her voice flat and cold. 'You are nothing to me now. Will you please remember that? Nothing at all.'

I stood there, staring at her, feeling pain eating into my heart.

'Why, sure,' I said. 'Congratulations, Gilda. You seem to have struck it pretty rich.'

121

'If you think you can blackmail me.' she said, and there was a vicious note in her voice that shocked me, 'you're mistaken. Don't try anything like that with me or you'll find out just how mistaken you are.'

'Blackmail you? Why should I blackmail you? Gilda: don't talk like that! I love you! I've never stopped thinking about you!'

'It was because of you I had to stand trial for my life,' she said, her forget-me-not blue eyes glittering. 'That's something I'll never forgive you for. Now get out!'

'But your husband wants me to build him a radiogram,' I said.

'I'll explain to my husband. Now get out! I'm not having you here! Get out and keep away from me!'

'All right,' I said, suddenly deflated. 'I won't bother you, Gilda. I'll keep away. I'd like to say I'm glad things have come out right for you. I wish you happiness.'

She turned her back on me and walked to the far end of the room and began to leaf through a magazine.

The butler let me out. I rode down in the express elevator too stunned to think or even feel.

Three weeks later I read in the newspaper of Henry Fuller's death.

He had fallen down the terrace steps of his roof garden and had broken his neck, There was to be an inquest.

Something that was morbid and frightening inside me urged me to go to the inquest.

The little courtroom was crowded with fashionably dressed people. I got a seat right at the back out of sight of those sitting up in front.

As I sat down I saw with a start of surprise that Maddox, of the National Fidelity was in the seat next to mine.

He gave me a sardonic grin as he nodded to me.

'Up on a business trip,' he said breezily. 'I thought I couldn't miss this performance, Well, well: history repeats itself, doesn't it? She's learning, and learning fast. The poor old dope wasn't insured, so she hasn't much to worry about.'

Before I could realize just what he was saying, Gilda came

in with George Macklin. She was in black and she looked lovely. She was pale and she held a handkerchief in her hand.

Macklin steered her to a chair. He seemed very solicitous and somehow possessive.

The Coroner treated her as if she were made of egg shells.

From the evidence there had been a party at Fuller's apartment. Most of the guests had been pretty high. Fuller had been drinking whisky and champagne all the evening, and he had been very unsteady on his legs. It had been a hot night, and the party had moved out into the roof garden after dinner.

There were thirty steps leading down to a second terrace. Most of the party had gone down there to get a closer look at the lights of the City.

Fuller and Gilda had remained at the top of the steps. Suddenly Fuller was seen to stumble. Then he fell. Gilda had made a desperate grab at his arm, but she had been too late.

He was dead when they reached him.

Maddox muttered to me, 'That's what I call a four million dollar push. A poor old drunk like Fuller would be child's play to her.'

There was no trouble about the verdict. Everyone had seen the accident. The Coroner was careful not to stress the fact that Fuller was drunk. He said apparently Fuller had become suddenly dizzy and had lost his balance. He expressed his sympathy for the widow, and then everyone drifted out, looking sorrowful.

Gilda was the first to leave. She didn't see me. She was holding her handkerchief to her eyes and Macklin, fussing a little, held her arm.

'Well, well,' Maddox said. 'Who says you can't get away with murder? Anyway, she never did get any money out of me.'

He nodded to me and went bustling down the steps and climbed into a taxi.

As I reached the street, I was in time to see Gilda and Macklin drive away in a big cream and blue Cadillac. She was looking at him, her face now bright and expectant, and he was leaning towards her, hanging on her words with that touch of

123

deference any up-and-coming attorney puts on when listening to a four million dollar client.

As I was walking back to the shop, for no reason at all, I suddenly remembered Delaney's words when he talked to me on the verandah so many weeks ago:

Do you know what's the matter with my wife? I'll tell you. She's mad about money. That's all she thinks about.

I paused, and stared blankly down the street.

Had she poisoned Delaney?

Had she pushed Fuller down the steps?

Had Maddox been right after all?

Then I remembered the softness of her body as she had lain in my arms, her forget-me-not blue eyes and her loveliness.

No, I said to myself, she wouldn't have done such a thing: not to Delaney, nor to Fuller.

I loved her.

How could I possibly believe such a thing about a woman I loved and would go on loving to the end of my days?

THE END

〉〉〉 If you've enjoyed this book and would like to discover more great vintage crime and thriller titles, as well as the most exciting crime and thriller authors writing today, visit: 〉〉〉

The Murder Room
Where Criminal Minds Meet

themurderroom.com